GW01418767

Nⓗoble
Rⓗomance

www.nobleromance.com

Shifters and Demons – The Vane, Book 1
ISBN 978-1-60592-262-1
ALL RIGHTS RESERVED
Copyright 2011 H.C. Brown
Cover Art by Fiona Jayde

H.C. Brown – The Vane, Book One, Shifters and Demons

Yours in Romance!

The Vane, Book One,

Shifters and Demons

Preface

1100 After Arious

Dragon's Gate

"I will not allow the Butcher of Anwyn to capture my bride." Prince Darik gathered up the reins of his prancing horse and glared at Lailii. "Do something, Spellweaver."

Lailii gathered her magyck about her and gazed intently at the cloud of dust surrounding the oncoming, mutant warriors. Heat shimmered across the desert sands, turning the approaching army into ethereal beings. She turned to her prince. "Yes, your majesty. Have no fear. I will ensure you have a safe journey to Mulway."

"See that you do." The prince nodded curtly, turned his horse, and motioned to his small contingent of men to retreat.

In the distance, the Butcher of Anwyn rode proudly before a battalion of the undead. With each second, the Army of Lost Souls moved closer. Even now, Lailii could see the red and yellow colors of the Butcher's standard. The ground trembled. Above, the sky darkened. Swirling sand had turned the twin, midday suns to blood red. A bad omen that heralded death and terror. Lailii's heart raced. Her magyck would hold the Butcher less than an hour. She took one last glance over her shoulder at the prince she had vowed to protect. He and his princess would be safe, but she would make the ultimate sacrifice.

With a toss of her head, Lailii opened her arms. *Goddess, give me strength.* Magyck crackled in the air. Dark Light shot from her fingertips. The smoky streamers fell over the soldiers, snuffing out all sense of direction, sight, and sound. The Army of Lost Souls ground to a confused halt.

As each long minute dragged by, Lailii knew the prince moved closer to the safe haven of Mulway. She bit her bottom lip and held her ground. With her nightscape, she gazed into the black void. The Butcher's men walked in circles or crawled in terror, mouths open in silent screams. *Just a little longer and my prince will be out of harm's way.* Her arms ached and her concentration waned. The constant flow of magyck drained her life force.

Without warning, the dark light collapsed, and the roar of the Army of Lost Souls beat down on her. The beasts would kill her and feast on her remains. Praying the intense spell would take her life, she gazed into the twisted faces growing closer by the second. The desert folded in on her, and she collapsed over the neck of her horse.

"You will not die today, Lailii of the Tark." The Butcher of Anwyn grabbed a handful Lailii's hair, dragged her from the horse, and threw her to the ground. "Lord Passio will grant me passage into the Underworld in exchange for you, Spellweaver."

In terror, Lailii kicked out at the man. She gagged at the smell pouring from his putrid mouth. Mutants surrounded her, blocking escape. The Butcher moved closer. An extra eye protruded from his cheek, flitting from side to side. She lifted her face to the twin suns to absorb a fraction of their power. Just a little magyck would gain her an advantage. The Butcher reached out one gnarled finger. Lailii scrambled to her feet. "Take your hands off me. I belong to Prince Darik."

"Oh, we are going to have so much fun with you. It will be some time before Lord Passio arrives." The Butcher pushed Lailii toward his men. "Hold her."

Lailii screamed. Strong hands tore at her clothes. She fought to find the power for one small spell to use against the disgusting beasts. The Butcher approached, stroking a huge, twin-headed cock, the massive, purple tips dripping with pre-cum. The mutants' misshapen hands dragged her legs apart and cheered encouragement to their leader.

The Butcher moved his twisted body between her legs. Lailii bucked to avoid the stream of drool leaking from the leader's mouth. The man grinned and bent to lick her exposed nipple, his long, pointed tongue circling the tip. *Goddess, help me.* Lailii drew on her diminished powers to send a sting of magyck to her captors. The mutants reacted in shocked surprise and dropped her onto the hot sand. She snarled and met the Butcher's gaze. "Any male who dares to rape me is *cursed.* His cock *will* turn black, shrivel, and fall off. *As so I will, so mote it be.*"

Chapter One

3,000 years later – 4100 After Arious
Lightening Falls Gate

Dallin inhaled the female's arousal and winked at Stryker. His lover lay on his back across the wide, black silk-covered bed. The sweetest Elfin female straddled his massive cock. They had hit gold this time. The willing female wanted both of them. After watching Stryker drive into her wet pussy for five long minutes, Dallin's balls ached. He reached for the tube of lube and approached the bed. He ran his tongue over his fangs. "May I have your ass, sweet thing?"

The female shot him a smile over her shoulder and pressed her small tits into Stryker's chest. Her sweet, white ass cheeks opened in invitation. Dallin groaned and applied lube to her inviting star. The female mewed her approval. Without hesitation, Dallin climbed onto the bed. He grasped his heavy cock and guided it into her tight hole with one thrust of his hips.

Taking a firm hold of her small waist, he drove into her. *So damn hot, so deliciously tight.* He gasped his thanks. With each plunge, he brushed Stryker's cock through the thin barrier of skin. What bliss. He met Stryker's hot gaze and knew they shared the same erotic experience. The touch, the slide of cock against cock, was intoxicating and one they both enjoyed.

Dallin's climax built quickly. The shivery sensations started in his belly, and the heat deep in his balls intensified with each delightful thrust. The room filled with the slap of bodies and the warm scent of sex. The female began to tremble, and then cried out her climax. She fell forward, spilling chestnut hair across Stryker's chest.

"Now, Dal." Stryker squeezed Dallin's thigh. "I'm gonna come."

With short, hard thrusts of his hips, Dallin drove into the female. Erotic sensations blurred his vision; white spots danced before his eyes. He gave into the bliss and spilled in delicious, hot spurts. Collapsing forward, he reached for Stryker and crushed the man's lips in a long, hot kiss. Gods, he loved the taste of the man.

"Oh, that is so sweet." The female rested her head on Striker's shoulder. "Can you get up now? You're crushing me."

After a long moment, Dallin broke the kiss. He glanced toward the digital readout flashing on the wall and swore. He rolled off the girl. "My father wants to see me." He looked down at the female. "How much, sweetheart?"

"For a new customer, the price is just one gold strip." The girl climbed off the bed and took a thumb scanner from her purse. "Each."

Dallin pressed his thumb on the device and grinned. "We'll call you again real soon. What was your name?"

"Rose. I work at the Freak Show most days." She licked her lips and smiled. "I can always bring a friend—male or female."

"I'll think on it." Dallin inclined his head toward the door. "You should leave now."

"What do you think the king wants?" Stryker slid off the bed and headed for the shower.

Dallin watched the girl pull on a long dress and leave. He closed the door behind her, and then followed Stryker into the shower. Turning to face his friend, he stared at the control panel sending a spike of magyck into the system. "I have no idea."

"Do you think he wants you to move back into the castle?" Stryker rubbed the back of his neck.

A blast of hot magyck swirled around them, and Dallin sighed. The *fresh and clean* glass cubicle did not compare to the satisfying experience of a hot shower. He turned around and grinned at his lover. "Well, it has been two years. He might—if he's forgiven me. To be honest, I wouldn't mind seeing my brothers again."

"I'll miss you." Stryker touched Dallin's arm. "You know I can't gain entrance to Vane Castle; will you come and visit me?"

With a chuckle, Dallin stepped from the cubicle and strode back into the bedroom. He went straight to the wardrobe and pulled out clean clothes. "You don't really think I could live without you, after three years of being together, do you? You are as close to me as any mate; we care for each other." He turned and smiled at Stryker. "I won't move anywhere without you."

"Good. Do you want me to come to the castle with you?" Stryker stood naked, his fists balled on his hips. "Or do you think the king will disapprove?"

"He knows about you already. We hardly hid the fact we were lovers. We were practically living together in my rooms at the castle." Dallin pulled on his clothes. "As long he knows I seek a female for my future queen, all will be well. My father had a lover, a Fae male named Sash, who died in the Mirra Uprising not long after I was born."

"Do you believe the Lady intends to find a mate for us to share?" Stryker pulled clothes from the chest of drawers and proceeded to dress.

Dallin pulled on his soft leather boots. He lifted his head to meet Stryker's deep, emerald gaze. The Talynx Pride male had the hard, muscular body of a seasoned warrior. Long, golden brown hair tumbled down his back in a waterfall of curls. Dallin loved his full lips, high cheekbones, and long, straight nose. As tall as Dallin, Stryker stood a good head and shoulders above most Pride males.

14

At the sight of his lover naked, Dallin grew hard again. *Gods, I can still taste him.* He could never have enough of the man. Dallin cleared his throat. "I have no doubt *we* were paired by the Lady. We have to trust She will guide us to the female of our dreams."

* * * * *

The street outside their modest home teemed with people. Market stalls lined both sides of the street, their brightly colored bunting giving the city of Lightning Falls a carnival atmosphere. Dallin cloaked, becoming invisible with a simple spell. No one in the sprawling metropolis knew the crown prince of the Vane lived within their midst. He followed Stryker through the crowd, weaving to avoid colliding with shoppers. They moved silently toward the parking lot. A stall containing necklaces of the rare, pink, Jaza crystals caught Dallin's eye. He stopped. "Wait, I want to buy something for my mom. I need an edge. She doesn't like me very much."

"Are you insane?" Stryker turned and searched the empty space behind him. "We need to keep moving."

"Buy the necklace shaped like a band of roses."

"Stay close; you'll have to use your thumb for the scanner. I don't have enough credits to pay for something that expensive." Stryker pushed the leaves of a potted plant to one side and stepped toward the stall.

"Can I help you, good sir?" The shopkeeper gave Stryker a wary look.

"Yes, I would like that one; wrap it up nicely for me." Stryker smiled warmly and pointed to the necklace.

Dallin moved closer and whispered in Stryker's ear. "In gold."

"Gold foil. Wrap it in gold." Stryker glared over his shoulder. "Happy now?"

They waited patiently for the shopkeeper to wrap the gift. The man fumbled the necklace many times with shaking fingers. Dallin bit his cheek to stop laughing. *He thinks Stryker belongs in a loony bin.* The purchase completed, Dallin slipped his thumb onto the scanner under Stryker's in a well-practiced move. With a chuckle, Dallin strode off toward his flybike. The sleek, silver vehicle sparkled under the afternoon sun. The lights on the front of the flybike flashed once, recognizing the arrival of its owner.

"You can't keep putting me in that position." Stryker climbed onto the flybike behind Dallin. "I already have the reputation of a sex-mad glutton. Now the word will be out that I speak to potted plants."

I love it. Dallin grinned into the sunshine. "The amount of money you spend, I doubt they would have the balls to say anything to upset you."

After pushing on his helmet, Dallin materialized. He zapped the engine, and the flybike shot high into the air. The sky was busy; silver bugs

17

peppered the airspace, carrying travelers from one city to another. Flybikes zipped between the tall, steel and glass high-rise city of magyck.

The trip to Vane Castle took them far away from the cities to the sandy coastline. Dallin breathed in the fresh sea air. In truth, his heart ached at being away from his home. He turned the flybike out to sea. The ocean drew him like an old friend, sending refreshing spray high into the air in welcome. The cat inside him roared its delight at the knowledge of going home. *Soon, cat. Soon we will hunt again.* His heart raced. The thought of being free to hunt in the forest as his ancestors had done for the past four thousand years filled him with joy.

Vane Castle sat on the craggy peak of Demon Island. Surrounded by a constant storm, massive waves, and tornadoes, the home of the Vane protected itself from intruders. Situated in the perpetual eye of the storm, Demon Island enjoyed a temperate climate all year round. Dallin pictured the picturesque village, the lush fields, and abundance of fruit trees. The disgusted expression on the face of his mother flashed across his mind, and he vividly recalled the angry tirade from his father the day the king banished him. *So he'd used his magyck to gain entrance to the females' baths – it was hardly a sin.*

As they approached the storm front, Dallin's gold armbands grew hot. The sacred magyck unlocked the protective shield for the crown prince. The black, rolling clouds parted, and Demon Island came into view. He dropped the flybike down to enjoy the panorama of the tropical island, gleaming like a jewel in the azure ocean. In the distance, Vane Castle sat like a black smudge against the cloudless, blue sky. He placed his hand on Striker's thigh. "It's good to be home."

Chapter Two

The castle grounds were alive with color and the scent of roses. Dallin dropped the flybike into the courtyard, and they dismounted. The king's guards surrounded them and escorted them to the great hall. The sound of boots hitting the hardwood floor echoed through the hallways. Dallin glanced around. Nothing had changed. The medieval castle remained the same. His father insisted the suits of armor and walls of ancient weaponry were to stay on display, even though they were out of place beside the large, flat information screens and modern furniture throughout the castle.

A few minutes later, they reached the great hall. Inside, voices rose in a heated discussion. Dallin glanced at Stryker and shrugged. "It sounds like they're arguing about me again."

The large, studded, oak doors swung open, and a footman announced their arrival. Dallin moved into the room with Stryker at his side. The red-faced king sat on a large, wing-backed chair surrounded by his advisors. Documents littered the table before them. No computers here – King Leopold relied on magyck alone. They walked toward the king and bowed. Dallin raised his chin and looked at his father. "You wanted to see me, father."

"So it would seem." The king got up slowly and rounded the table to stand before his son. "The Oracle insists the Lady has a mission for you and your lover. You are to go to the grotto at daybreak, and pray for guidance."

Dallin rubbed the back of his neck. His father had lost his mind. Who believed the Oracle in these days of enlightenment? He met the king's amethyst gaze. "I hardly think the Lady would counsel me. I'm a sinner—as you have told me most eloquently in the past."

"You are forgiven." The king opened his arms, palms up. "It is the only way to stop my advisors from pestering me. I want you to move into the castle and take up your duties as Crown Prince. "

With a wide grin, Dallin stepped forward and offered his arm to his father. The king smiled weakly and clasped Dallin's arm. The old man tipped his white head toward Stryker. Dallin followed his gaze. "You *do* remember my lover, Stryker of Talynx."

"Yes, I do." The king turned his full attention on Stryker. "What is your talent?"

"I have many talents, sire." Stryker inclined his head respectfully. "My main talent is dream weaving."

"Yes, I expected such from your lineage." The king rubbed his chin. "Your grandmother is a Faerie, if I'm not mistaken?"

"She is, sire."

"Good, good. You are welcome in my home, Stryker of Talynx." The king turned to Dallin. "When you are settled, I have arranged entertainment for you at the waterfall. Dinner is at eight, as usual."

Dallin ran a hand through his hair. "First, I would like to see mother, and where are my brothers?"

"They're hunting in Bree Forest. They will return home this evening. Your mother is in my solar, waiting for you. Go to her now; the woman has been driving me insane with her insistence to see you the second you arrived." The king waved his hand in dismissal.

Stryker followed Dallin from the great hall. His stomach unclenched. Lady's blood, he had met King Leopold. The leader of all the Prides within the lands of the Twelve Gates had accepted him into his home. The days of sneaking from the barracks to meet Dallin were over. Gods, be praised.

With a grin, he took in the man walking beside him. The crown prince was the epitome of a Vane, the ruling Pride of white tiger shifters. Massive in build, he walked with authority. Black hair fell like water to brush his shoulders. The silken mass framed a face only a god could have created, to hold amethyst eyes flecked with green and silver opalescence. Stryker's gaze dropped from Dallin's broad shoulders to his trim waist, and then down to strong thighs cased in a skintight material, woven by the Fae to resemble leather. He knew the feel of those strong thighs pressing against him. One whiff of his lover's unique scent sent him into rapture. He touched his lips at the memory of Dallin's demanding kiss. The taste of the prince lingered on his tongue.

"Do you mind if I see her alone?" Dallin stopped at the top of a flight of stairs. "I have some crawling to do."

Drawn from his thoughts, Stryker blinked. He cleared his throat and met Dallin's gaze. "Sure. I'll hang around and wait. What do you think the king has planned for us at the waterfall?"

"I'm guessing hot, pride females and a ménage ceremony." Dallin winked. "My father may be old but he does encourage us to have frequent sex with a variety of females. How else would a male learn to cope with a female in Moonfire? One needs experience. It's the same in most Prides."

Stryker nodded in agreement. "I agree, but it's after the mating that troubles me. My father insists all will be well, but do you honestly believe one female will satisfy us both?"

"After we bite our chosen mate and she us, all desire for another will fade." Dallin placed a hand on Stryker's shoulder. "It is the Lady's way. Once our childseed is released we are bound to one female for life."

They moved along a passageway with windows down one side. At the end, two guards stood to attention. The open door to the king's solar revealed a large, opulent room. The queen sat beside a massive, marble fireplace, her feet encased in red slippers supported by a large, blue silk cushion. She glanced toward the door, and her face creased in a wide ˌsmile. Dallin threw a mischievous grin at Stryker and strode into the room, closing the door behind him.

The guards' stony expressions remained neutral; only their eyes flicked toward Stryker. He turned and rested his head on the windowpane. His breath clouded the view of the spectacular rose garden below. With a sigh, he straightened his shoulders and looked out on the familiar landscape. So much had happened since his father sent him to train as a warrior in the king's army. Well, in truth, the king offered him the chance to ride with the elite Vane Patrol after he defeated six of his warriors in a mock battle. Stryker grinned. At eighteen, he thought he was invincible – until he met Dallin.

Friendship followed the long training sessions at Vane Castle. Stryker's heart missed a beat. The memory of becoming Dallin's lover was still fresh in his mind. He grew hard, and turned away from the guards. Hell, that night had branded his lust meter for all time. Okay, like most Pride males of their age, they liked to share females, rolling off one and then onto the other. That night, only one female came to Dallin's bedchamber. The thrill of them taking her, both at the same time, had blown his mind. The first brush of thighs, the touch of cock against cock, and then the first hot, wet kiss had sealed their fate.

The memory of the king's displeasure and harsh words to Dallin at the request for a ménage ceremony ran through Stryker's mind. "*Just because you want a male's ass, doesn't mean a lifetime commitment. This public declaration for a Talynx male is unnecessary. You will tire of him soon enough.*"

Stryker smiled to himself. The stolen nights together that followed had proven Dallin's devotion. They had discovered every possible way to satisfy each other, and now he grew hard with one sultry look from the man. Hell, the prince was a wet dream walking.

The door to the solar opened, and Dallin gave Stryker a wink and beckoned him forward. Stryker ran a hand through his hair. With his heart threatening to burst through his chest, he followed his lover into the room. He bowed low before the queen. She got to her feet and tipped her head to one side, wearing a bemused expression. Stryker's face grew hot. *Gods, I hope she hasn't noticed my erection.*

"So this is the one who took my son's virginity." The queen raised a brow. "What are you?"

"I am Talynx Pride, madam."

"A silver lynx . . . ." Her small hands fisted at her waist. "I must insist you visit the King of the Fae to blend your cats once mated. My son is crown prince. It will not do for his mate to produce anything but a white tiger for his heir. The Vane *is* the white tiger."

Anger cut through Stryker as sharp as a knife. He met the queen's gaze. "I will trust the Lady to blend our childseed, madam. I believe our cats are compatible."

"Do you believe the inferior lynx should blend with our royal blood?" The queen's lip curled. "Look at you—more Fae than Pride."

Dallin moved closer to Stryker. The man's eyes flashed with anger; any second now, he would morph. He touched his lover's arm. "The Talynx blending with the Fae was by the Lady's design, Mother. Their magyck is known throughout the realms." He met his mother's angry gaze. "His cat is as big as my own. Stryker is my choice—I believe he is the Lady's choice for me."

"Then for the gods' sake, chose a tiger for your mate. Our pride will not accept a half breed for their king." The queen turned her back. "It is a shame the beautiful gift you brought me is tarnished by this unhappy news."

After staring at his mother's hunched back for a few long seconds, Dallin sighed. "It has been many years since I visited the Lady's grotto. In the morning, I will pray for you, Mother. Pray that the Lady forgives you for doubting Her choice for me."

Without another word, he led Striker out of the room and down the stairs. Two squires stood in the hallway. They bowed and waited for Dallin to speak. He looked at the young men and grinned. "Jon and Matt, how good to see you again. Look at you. You must be of age now. Why aren't you attending me?"

"We are not squires, sir." Jon pushed back a strand of blond hair. "We are nineteen summers now and in the king's guard."

"Your new squires wait to serve you in your chamber, sir." Matt dropped his gaze. "We are part of this afternoon's entertainment. You are to witness our rite of ménage."

Dallin grew hard, his shaft pressed uncomfortably against the front of his pants. It had been a long time since he witnessed such an event.

The chance to watch two virgin males experience their first taste of sex would be erotic bliss. He shot a glance at Stryker, and the man returned a hot gaze. *Oh yeah, this is going to be one great homecoming.* "I'll look forward to it."

The men moved off, and Dallin dragged Stryker into an alcove. Surprised the passion could rise so quickly, he pushed the man's back against the wall and crushed his lips. His lover responded, grasping handfuls of Dallin's hair and then opening his mouth for the kiss. Dallin rubbed his heavy cock against Stryker's erection. Their tongues danced, explored in a desperate need to get closer. The scent of the man infused his senses; he tasted like ambrosia. Dallin dragged his head away and tried desperately to draw a breath. "They'll expect us to fuck the chosen females. It will be difficult when right now all I want is you."

"We'll have all night." Stryker nibbled a path along Dallin's jaw. "But I won't be happy if you take one of the males."

Dallin snorted. "I have no interest in other males; *you* have bewitched me."

"Remember that when you watch the ceremony." Stryker met Dallin's gaze. "Those untried boys look tempting."

"*You* are all I need. I've not touched another male since we met." Dallin grinned. "But, I will take my fill of the females. I hope to share some of them with you."

"Well then, what are we waiting for?" Stryker pushed away from the wall. "Lead the way, my prince."

Dallin led the way through the castle and out onto a secluded, rock plateau. A bubbling waterfall cascaded from the rock face, sending rainbows in all directions. The blue, crystal-clear water fed a massive rock pool high on a ridge on the west side of the castle. Surrounded by palm trees and fragrant blossoms, the relaxation area was an oasis against the black granite mountain. Dallin stopped at the entrance and gazed around. Naked females lounged on large, flat rocks or splashed in the pool. He grinned to himself, recalling the sweet memory of his own ceremony.

Built for lovemaking, with secluded areas for the shy and padded benches for the exhibitionists, the waterfall cavern catered to every taste. Servants served food and wine. An assortment of tables supplied the orgy with every type of aphrodisiac lube and toy available. Dallin grinned and strode into the changing rooms. Today, the young males would prove their stamina by taking many females and submitting to a variety of males. He could not wait.

Dallin slapped Stryker on the back. "My cock is aching. Hurry and strip off so we can join in the fun."

"Did you notice the female with the huge tits lying on the rock?" Stryker ripped off his pants. "And the one twisting her hair around her finger—fuck, that turns me on something wicked."

Running his tongue over his fangs, Dallin moaned. "Can you imagine what it would feel like to bite during sex? Can one die from the pleasure-pain of releasing venom, the ecstasy of a mate's bite? I wonder if it hurts when childseed fills our balls or if it's bliss."

"I've heard only good things, although, no mated male reveals the entire truth. It is far too personal to recount like a dirty story." Stryker grinned. "Mind you, I get my thrills running my fangs across your balls."

"Mmm, so do I."

They undressed and headed for the pool. Dallin dived into the warm water and surfaced beside Stryker. They swam a couple of lengths together, and then climbed onto a rock to stretch out side by side. Dallin rolled over onto his stomach and rested on his elbows. From here, they had a good view of the padded benches favored for the ceremony. He glanced at Stryker. "Do you remember our ceremony?"

"Sure." Stryker gave Dallin a slow smile. "We kinda broke from convention though, didn't we?" He chuckled. "It was like the blind leading the blind."

Dallin snorted. "I *knew* what I was doing. Fuck, we'd both had quite a few females by then, not like these two." He tipped his head toward Jon and Matt, who stood in the center of the complex, their faces beet red. "Although, I must admit, it was a little unconventional to have a virgin for my first male lover and vice versa."

"And to insist no other males be involved." Stryker met Dallin's gaze. "I liked that—just you and me."

A head broke through the water. The man shook his long, black hair. Water cascaded down his sun-bronzed skin. Dallin grinned. "Cruz. Hey, man, I thought you were out hunting."

"What, and miss the chance of meeting the visiting females? You have to be joking." Cruz nodded a greeting to Stryker. "I heard your brother mated a Human. Fuck, aren't they riddled with disease?"

"So I hear, but they must be transformed before they can travel through the Gates." Stryker shrugged.

"No illness can survive Pride venom. Sue is Pride now. Her Human life is behind her."

"Well, that's a relief." Cruz turned his head to look at two females across the pool. "I'm going to sit with the twins; catch you later. Don't worry. I'm leaving as soon as I convince the twins to party in my room. I'm sure you don't want me around." He swam off in the direction of two dark-haired beauties lounging on a large, flat rock.

"Do princes *have* to take part in a ménage ceremony?" Stryker watched Dallin's brother swim away. "I don't recall hearing about Cruz's ceremony."

Dallin chuckled. "He hasn't had one. It's not compulsory. Cruz likes the girls just as much as we do. He is such an exhibitionist. I'm betting if he finds a male to ride him, he'll be holding a ceremony." He grimaced. "It's not something I want to see. In fact, I'm glad he'll be leaving soon."

A gong sounded, and the rush of water became the only noise in the cavern. Matt, his entire body flushed, chose to be standing with wrists bound and attached to an overhead bar. Dallin groaned. He would love to fuck Stryker just like that. A female approached and kissed Matt long and hard. She dragged her nails down the virgin's body and stepped to one side. Dallin recognized the two men standing in the shadows, both lieutenants in the royal guard. Matt would take one of them as his lover and both would enjoy a host of females, as was the custom.

One of the lieutenants pressed his naked body against Matt's broad back. The male's hands caressed Matt's body, pinching his flat nipples. Matt turned his head. His face flushed, and he kissed his lover in a long, slow kiss, hot enough to melt steel. Dallin grew hard, his cock pressing against the rock.

The girl fell to her knees, dragging her nails down Matt's hips. She licked a wet path up the inside of the young Pride's thighs, and then sucked his balls. When she pushed open Matt's legs and applied lube to his anal star, Dallin rolled on his side and grasped his aching cock. His gaze followed Matt's shaft into her willing mouth. He flicked his attention to the young man's face. The lieutenant continued his attention with long, passionate kisses.

Two females, Holly and Reba, climbed onto the rock bedside Dallin. He grinned at the pair. "Well, your timing is spot on, ladies."

Holly gave him a sweet smile and bent her blonde head to take his heavy cock into her mouth. Her mouth was so damn hot, so wet, and the scrape of her fangs almost undid his control. Dallin gasped and turned to watch Reba pleasure Stryker. He glanced back to the ceremony in time to see the lieutenant grasp Matt's hips and drive into him. The crowd in the cavern cheered at Matt's cry of fulfillment.

Lady's blood, Holly was good at this; the female circled Dallin's ass with her thumb, and gods bless her, bobbed her head to mimic the lieutenant's thrusts. Dallin rolled his hips, pushing deep into her soft mouth.

The need to taste Stryker overwhelmed him. Dallin locked his legs around Holly and rolled over to claim Stryker's full lips. His lover's fervid response shot straight to his balls. All control disappeared in a rush of erotic pleasure. He let himself go and came in a long shudder. To his delight, Stryker sighed in his mouth, reaching his own climax. Dallin opened his eyes to meet the man's emerald gaze. "Now that was sweet."

Stryker blinked, surprised at this public display of affection. Since their ceremony, Dallin had insisted they keep their relationship private. Reba enthusiastically licked him clean, and then pressed warm kisses up his chest. Then she pressed her full breasts against him. He raised a brow at Dallin. "And so unexpected, my prince."

"My father gave us his blessing." Dallin drew Holly close to his side. "Now, all we need to do is find a mate." He grinned wolfishly. "I believe we may need to sample many before we find the Lady's gift."

The cat inside Stryker roared. The need to find a mate had become critical. *Hush, cat, I will be guided by your knowledge. If the prince's mate is not ours too, we will find one of our own.*

With a smile, Stryker rolled Reba onto her back and kissed her. Her long legs curled around his hips. He lifted his head and grinned at Dallin. "I think I'd like to do my sampling on a soft bed. This rock is murder on the knees."

"Sure, after the ceremony." Dallin bent to suckle Holly's nipple.

A cheer went up, and Stryker turned his attention toward the bench in the middle of the cavern. Jon, with crimson cheeks and an expression of pure bliss, lay on his back on the bench. He had his fingers buried in the hair of the slim female bobbing up and down his cock. Jon's muscular legs rested on the broad shoulders of the other lieutenant. The man, with sweat running off his chin, fucked Jon hard; the sound of their bodies slapping together vibrated around the cavern.

"You know I don't remember my first time being that good." Dallin chuckled. "How come you didn't get some sweet thing to give me head when you did the deed?"

Stryker rubbed the back of his neck. His heart sank. *Now that's a low blow.* He looked at Dallin's mischievous grin. *Gods, he's joking.* "I was just following your lead."

"Good, then follow my lead outta here." Dallin jumped into the water, dragging Holly with him. He surfaced and grinned at Stryker. "We have almost four hours before dinner."

Chapter Three

The following morning, Dallin awoke to the sound of tapping on the door. He nuzzled Stryker under the ear, breathing in the familiar scent of his lover. "There's someone at the door."

"Tell them to leave us alone." Stryker mumbled, burying his face in the pillow.

The knocking became more insistent.

"I have to go to the Lady's grotto this morning. That will be my squire," Dallin said.

"I hope he brought breakfast." Stryker rolled over and pushed the hair out of his eyes. He glanced down at his nakedness. "Do you have some clothes I can borrow?"

Dallin rubbed his thumb across Stryker's swollen lips. The man had true Pride libido. Hell, they had made love five times during the night. He could still taste him. "Sure, take what you need. I gave orders for our things to be brought here; they should arrive today."

"Good." Stryker slid off the bed and walked toward the bathroom. He stopped in the doorway and turned. "I hope they fed the Loop."

An image of the sleek, catlike creature crossed Dallin's mind. His pet since childhood hated Stryker with a Passion. "Her *name* is Buzz, and you know it. I left her plenty of food. She will love living back in the castle. I have no idea why you dislike each other. She's a sweet, little thing."

"I have other words for a four-eyed, venomous, psychopathic bitch with two-inch talons." Stryker shot Dallin a look of disgust.

He chuckled at Stryker's stream of expletives and turned his attention to the hammering at the door. "Enter."

A young squire entered, followed by servants bearing food. Dallin waited for the squire to make his bow and bit back a laugh at the boy's attire — red vest, knee-length breeches, and white stockings, like something out of the dark ages. Gods, his father lived 3000 years behind the times. "Good morning. What is your name?"

"Good morning, sir. My name is George. I am your day squire. Peter will care for you in the evening."

Dallin slithered out of bed and walked slowly to the shower. He grinned. All the servants lowered their gaze. *My nakedness offends them.* "What if I want *you* to look after me at night, George?"

"My father requires I be at home for the evening meal, sir." George moved around nervously. He lifted his gaze for a split second. "But I would be honored to serve you in any capacity."

I'll give the kid a break. "Daytime is fine. Lay out two sets of clothes." Dallin leaned casually against the doorframe. "I prefer to eat my breakfast in the sitting room, and in future, don't wake me unless there's a war."

"Yes, sir." George took two steps toward Dallin and paused. "Do you wish me to bathe you, sir?"

Dallin pushed away from the doorframe and threw the boy a wide grin. "No, thanks. I've lived without a squire for the past two years, so as long as you see to my chambers, clothes, and food, we will get along just fine."

* * * * *

Later that morning, Dallin entered the courtyard with Stryker at his side. As he passed through the castle, servants fell to their knees and buried their heads in the dirt. Dallin found the practice more than a little uncomfortable. "I can't understand why my father insists they prostrate themselves like this; it's so demeaning. It's not as if we have any hold on them. They are employees — not bloody slaves."

"They do it out of respect for you." Stryker brushed a bumblebee off his shoulder. "Shit, the insects think this yellow shirt is a daffodil."

I believe all men are equal. Dallin growled. "When I become king, I'll insist a nod is sufficient recognition. I appreciate their respect, but it can be shown in other ways."

"What is upsetting you?" Stryker threw Dallin a worried look. "I've seen you less aggressive going into battle. Surely, visiting the Lady's grotto isn't such a problem."

They followed the paved walkway to the postern gate and took the secluded path to the Lady's grotto. Dallin stopped at the gate and turned to his friend. "It's not my faith; I *believe* in the Lady. But you know that only the Pride king may enter this sacred place." He scrubbed both hands over his face. "My father once told me the Lady appeared to him, to guide him. All these years, I've wondered if he spoke the truth." He rested a hand on Stryker's shoulder. "Now he tells me the Lady requested my presence. It goes against thousands of years of Pride tradition for a prince to enter. I fear this visit will prove my father lied."

"Have faith he speaks the truth." Stryker squeezed Dallin's arm. "Go, there is one way to find out. I'll be here, waiting, even if it takes all day."

Dallin let his gaze travel around the rose garden surrounding the impressive, white marble building. The roses here flowered all year round; in fact, he knew the flowers never wilted or died. No leaves fell from the overhead canopy of trees. Inside the wrought iron fence, peacocks strutted, their brilliant feathers erect. Lorikeets fed on bushes laden with berries, and butterflies moved in colorful swarms from bloom to bloom.

With a sigh, Dallin pushed open the gate and stepped inside the garden. His boots crunched on the crushed-marble walkway. He walked through the archway and paused inside the vestibule to wash his hands and face in the gold bowl of holy water. The entrance to the grotto shimmered in a stream of mercury, like the travel Gates, although no destination reflected in its depths. Panic gripped his belly. *I'm such a fool. The Lady won't kill me for doing my father's bidding.*

Drawing a deep breath, he stepped forward into a small room. The subdued light calmed his nerves. He glanced around — apart from a bench and a potted bush of the most exquisite, solid gold roses, the room was empty. Dallin moved toward the bench, sat down, and closed his eyes. *Dear Lady, I am here for your guidance on my father's request.*

"Open your eyes, Dallin of the Vane."

A spike of terror ran down Dallin's back. His eyes shot open, and he glanced around the empty room. Had he imagined the voice in his head? "Madam, I hear you."

A swirl of blue smoke curled from the flagstones. The iridescent vapor twirled in a vortex, and the ghostly image of a woman appeared. Dallin gasped. Never in all his life had he seen such beauty. Her expression held deep compassion, and her eyes melted his heart. He tried to draw a breath to speak to the vision. For that moment, her presence struck him dumb.

"Dallin, you were born to become my champion – to do my bidding for the good of all in the Lands of the Nine Gates. Many thousands of years have passed since I gave a mortal this acknowledgement." The Lady floated up and down, wringing her hands. *"My task for you is great. I have a child, Lailii of the Tark, imprisoned in a land 3000 years in your past. I commission you to take an army and rescue her, bring her into the future."*

Dallin ran a hand through his hair. Gods, the Lady was *real,* and she was speaking to *him.* "How do I travel into the past? How will I know where to find Lailii?"

"The Butcher of Anwyn has her in his dungeon at Dragon Gate. She grows weak. This evil being is in league with Passio, lord of the Underworld. Passio wants to use Lailii to enhance his position and power. The demon knows no passage of time, and on your return, he may yet find her here. You will protect the girl from the demon. From this day forth, I deliver her into your care."

"Dear Lady, I am mortal and no match for a demon."

"You are my champion – you will forever carry my mark. The child is weak, too weak to travel. I will instill your venom with healing properties. Stryker is my other choice for you; together you will bite Lailii and make her strong – make her Pride. Make ready. In two days, a Gate will open beside my garden. You will take a battalion on horseback to the Butcher's castle. Do what is necessary to retrieve the girl. The future of the Prides depends on her

safety. Return to your point of origin to access the Gate home."

Dallin blinked twice. The image faded into mist. He sat for some moments, head in hands, trying to assimilate the information. He had not expected this monumental occurrence. Gods, it was five years since he sat on a horse let alone rode one into battle. Shit, now he realized his consuming desire to learn to fight with a broadsword. This must have been Her plan for his lifetime. He rubbed his chin. There must be some way to take a zap into the past. He could not possibly expect his troops to fight with swords. He got to his feet and walked to the rose bush. He touched the crafted, metal petals and inhaled their delicate perfume. A warm glow of peace flowed through him, instilling strength and conviction. *That is amazing.*

With one last glance around the room, he turned on his heel and left the grotto. He stepped outside into twilight. How long had he been inside, five or maybe ten minutes? What the hell was going on? Stryker sat, leaning against a tree, feet crossed at the ankles. He gave Dallin a cheeky grin. Dallin pushed open the gate and walked over to him. The man had a large basket filled with food and wine at his side. "Well, you look happy. What time is it?"

"Almost six, you've been inside for eight hours." Stryker yawned. "This basket appeared about at lunchtime, and no matter how much I eat it keeps replenishing. I didn't know you could do this magyck."

"I can't." Dallin sank to the grass beside him and reached inside the basket for a chicken leg. "It's not my magyck. I'm guessing it's from the Lady. I thought I was inside for ten minutes, max. She is real. I saw her with my own two eyes."

"Can you tell me what she said?" Stryker pointed to Dallin's upper arm. "And what the hell is that?"

Dallin looked down at his arm. Above the gold armband, a gold motif glittered on his skin. He pulled his arm around and saw a circle of leaves surrounding a gold rosebud. As he watched, the petals opened and then slowly closed. He shot Stryker a grin. "It's the Lady's mark. I'm her champion, and we have a mission."

They ate slowly while Dallin recounted the Lady's story. Dallin tossed the empty bottle of Miza wine into the basket and brushed the crumbs from the front of his shirt. He met Stryker's gaze with a smile. "She said you were chosen for me."

"Was there any doubt?" Stryker chuckled. "I don't suppose She mentioned our mate, did She?"

Dallin shrugged. "No." He rubbed the back of his neck. "To be honest, I find biting a child and changing her to Pride a bit sick. But if that's what we need to do to save her life then we do it, I guess."

"We are *all* the Lady's children. I believe it is a figure of speech." Stryker picked a blade of grass and rolled it in his fingers. "A child would hardly pose a threat to the Butcher of Anwyn—my guess is that she is no child and has one hell of a power." He flicked the grass away. "Our problem will be convincing her that we're on her side."

They walked back to the courtyard, and a pair of dancing stallions confronted them. The grooms battled to control the magnificent warhorses. Dallin moved closer. "By the gods, I thought all the war horses were extinct."

The horses calmed. One glossy, black beast walked toward Dallin and nuzzled his arm. The white did likewise to Stryker. The grooms watched the docile animals in amazement. Dallin ran his hand down the horse's nose. The names of the horses drifted through his mind. "This is Courage and yours is Glory."

"A gift from the gods." Stryker patted his mount. "I've never seen a horse this size."

"There are twenty more in the stables." The groom handed Dallin the reins. "The king has trained his troops on horseback for the past six months. They, like you, my lord, have also become proficient in swordplay."

"How convenient." Dallin handed back the reins. "Have the horses saddled first thing in the morning so I may put the troops through their paces." He ran a hand through his hair. "Take a message to the Master of Arms. Tell him we ride to war in two days—with zaps."

"Yes, sir." The groom took Courage and led him toward the stable.

Dallin gazed at the two retreating beasts. The puzzle was falling into place. His father must know about the mission. Had known for six months and yet left it to the last minute to recall him to Demon Island. Sadness overwhelmed him. The forgiveness he craved had not brought him home after all.

Chapter Four

1100 After Arious
Dragon's Gate

Darkness surrounded Lailii. She battled to live through never-ending nights of despair, broken only with the scatter of rats across the damp floor. They would eat her alive—she knew it. The second she stopped fighting against the sharp teeth gnawing at her toes, she would die.

56

The Butcher left her alone in her misery, bound in silver to prevent her using her powers. She sat amid her own waste with only a crust of stale bread, and a flagon of water to quench her thirst. For the first three months, every time the door to the cell ground open, she hoped Prince Derik had arrived to save her. Now she knew the guard that pushed the food inside the door would be the last face she saw before she died. The prince had deserted her and left her to perish. She lifted her head and gazed into the darkness. *Dear Lady, I beg you, show mercy, take me through the veil.*

"Hold fast, child, for I have sent my Champion."

Lailii shook her head. She had finally gone mad. Now voices invaded her mind. Curling her arms around her knees, she rocked, the clang of the chains a refreshing change from the silence. Surely, death would follow madness. She welcomed it and tried to picture open fields, flowers and seascapes. If she must die in this filth, she would die with her mind filled with beauty.

Sometime later, high above the dungeon, she could hear the faint cries of men. Just of late, an eerie quiet had surrounded the castle. The usual sounds of troops in battle practice the only difference between night and day. Perhaps the Butcher had returned. She straightened her shoulders at the thought. No matter how weak she became, she would fight the bastard until her last breath.

The door to the dungeon flew open. A blast of light burned her eyes. The Angel of Death, bathed in a golden halo, filled the doorway. The huge man, encased in glistening gold armor, moved toward her. Lailii pushed her back against the wall, her mouth opened in a silent scream.

"Lady's blood, it stinks like death in here. For fuck's sake, tell me you are Lailii of the Tark." The angel aimed a metal stick at her. "I guess you are. No one else is alive down here. Hold still while I remove the chains."

Lailii pressed her hand over her mouth. She froze. A white-hot beam shot from the stick and sliced the chain like butter. The angel lifted her and threw her over one broad shoulder. She fluttered against his armor like a towel in the breeze.

"Best you keep your eyes shut until I can get you upstairs. The light will burn your retinas." The angel took the steps two at a time. "You are safe now. I am Dallin, the Lady's champion."

Her savior, Dallin, moved swiftly through the castle. Lailii chanced a glance. Her vision blurred, then came into focus. The castle was in disarray, tables and chairs smashed to pieces. She blinked. Tears stung her eyes. *Dear Lady.* She gasped. Bile rushed up the back of her throat. The floor beneath Dallin's boots ran red with blood.

"Keep your eyes shut, little one. The carnage will rot your soul." Dallin patted Lailii's bottom. "My men are drawing water for a bath for you. I am here to protect you from the Butcher. We will leave this place as soon as you can travel. The Army of Lost Souls is three day's march from here."

Lailii could not close her eyes. It had been so long since she had seen anything but darkness. She took in the tired faces of men dragging dead bodies into a pile. The battle to save her had been fierce. Other, strangely dressed warriors helped the injured. Her eyes burned, and her head throbbed from bumping up and down on Dallin's armor.

Dallin turned into a darkened bedchamber and lowered Lailii to the floor. He gazed at her emaciated body and swallowed hard. The kid was in bad shape. Fuck, she was so thin. There was not much of her neck left to bite. The smell was overpowering. With one swift movement, he ripped her dress down the front, pulled it off her body, and tossed it into the fire. He lifted her and set her gently into a tub of warm, scented water. She cried out in pain the second the water hit the open sores on her delicate wrists. He handed her a bar of soap and a rag. "You start. I'll remove my armor and help you."

He stood and turned to Stryker. "Got anything to get this stink off me?"

"Yes, boss." Stryker grinned. "We brought heaps." He poured disinfectant over a cloth and began to wipe Dallin's armor. "There you go."

Dallin used his magyck to collapse the armor. It folded down and crumpled into a tiny square. He picked up the gold package and slipped it into his pants pocket. He turned his gaze back on the girl. She looked at him with the most amazing silver eyes, not blue but rather pure silver. Waist-length, platinum hair stuck out under a coat of filth. Her face was ethereal. She looked like a wood nymph.

A sudden pang of compassion hit Dallin, and he turned and dismissed his men from the room. The poor kid looked terrified. There was no need to put her on exhibition for his troops. He turned to Stryker. "I'll hold her, you remove the silver. What an asshole to use silver on a child. Look at the damage to her wrists."

"I'm not a child, good sir." Lailii covered her breasts with the rag. "I am a fully grown woman of nineteen summers." She met Dallin's gaze. "I may *look* like a child, but even a man of your bulk would diminish if starved to death for six months."

Dallin raised a brow. "Now I know how you survived. You've got guts, lady."

"I am no lady." Lailii held out her wrists for Stryker to remove the silver bands. "I am Lailii of the Tark, Spellweaver for Prince Derik."

"You are the Spellweaver for Prince Dallin now, little one, *spoils of war.*"

"If you think to rape me, think again." Lailii glared at Dallin. "I will curse you."

Lady give me strength. Dallin turned to Stryker and crossed his eyes. "What do you think, Stry, fancy a tumble with the skinny wench?"

"Nah, I think I'll give her a miss." He grinned. "We might break her."

With a sigh, Dallin removed his shirt. The Lady insisted he care for the girl, so he would. He kneeled beside the tub. Lailii shrank back, her eyes wide with terror. Dallin smiled and poured glamor over her. She reacted immediately. Lailii blinked her angry, silver eyes and slapped him hard across the face. He stared at her in disbelief. "What was that for?"

"You think to use glamor on me? How *dare* you." She pouted. "And it is not dignified for a male to disrobe in front of a maiden." She pointed at the gold mark on Dallin's arm. "And pray tell, what is that strange, gold mark on your arm?"

Rubbing his cheek, Dallin rolled back on his heels. "Okay, little one, let's get this straight. The Lady sent me to get you. I wear Her mark." He sighed. "I do not intend to hurt you in any way." He held his hand over his heart. "I promise, and Stryker promises too. Now allow me to help you wash your hair. My men are searching for clothes for you. As soon as you are clean, we can leave this awful place."

"I'll go and check on the men." Stryker turned and headed for the door. He threw Dallin a grin. "Make sure you scrub her neck."

Dallin laughed, and the girl screamed. He turned to look at her. "What now?"

"You have fangs. Lady help me, you *are* demons." Lailii stood up in the tub, her knees trembling.

"We are Pride from 3000 years in the future." Dallin pushed Lailii down in the tub. "Sit while I wash your hair."

To Dallin's relief, the girl sat motionless while he soaped her knotted hair. By the time he poured the last bucket of water over her head, she had relaxed. He stood and opened a large, linen sheet. Without a complaint, she stepped into his arms, and he began to dry her. Her back pressed against his chest. He glanced at the door, willing Stryker to enter. This would be the perfect time to bite her. It would have to be a surprise. Dallin doubted the female would submit willingly. He smiled to himself at the ingenuity of his plan.

The Lady had said his bite would heal. Once bitten, the girl would know he meant no harm. When she was fitter, they could both bite her and turn her into a Pride female. She would blend in with his people and be safe from Passio. He pulled her close, drew a deep breath, and sank his fangs into her neck.

"What are you doing to me?" Lailii struggled. "*Arh.*"

The taste of her blood ran across his tongue like ambrosia. His face hurt. Venom filled the sacs in his cheeks and exploded through his fangs. The erotic delight sent flames of passion to his balls. He grew hard and unconsciously ground his heavy shaft into her back. Lailii fell limp in his arms. Under his palms, her heart pounded. Gods, each suck hit him like a climax. His cat screamed in his head. "*Mine*"

He dragged his mouth away and fought the overpowering need to mate. *No cat, we bite her to make her strong.*

"Mine." The cat insisted.

Dallin held the female at arm's length and stared into her pale face. "Are you okay?"

Lailii trembled. What had just happened? These deep feelings of lust were most unfamiliar. She pulled the sheet around her body and looked into Dallin's face. Such a handsome face. Indeed, both he and Stryker were outstanding. She rubbed her neck. The touch of Dallin's mouth had sent shivers down her spine. Her entire body tingled from his touch. She drew in the scent of him; these small offerings of delight charged her powers. Gods, his kiss could recharge her magyck completely. Mayhap the Lady had sent him to her, for indeed, her body grew stronger by the second.

She tugged at the knots in her hair. "Why did you bite me? I was fearful, but I must say it was not an unpleasant experience."

"My venom will make you strong." Dallin dropped his arms, and then bent to pick up his clothes. "You should prepare yourself, as both Stryker and I will need to bite you simultaneously before we leave."

With a frown, Lailii met his gaze. "Why?"

"To travel into our realm, you will need to become one of us. The Lady's instructions were to bite you. Our venom will change you."

"The Butcher will hunt me down. You don't understand; he is the right hand of the demon, Passio."

"We are fully aware of the Butcher and his allegiance. You'll be safe. I promised the Lady I'd protect you. I keep my word, little one." He pulled on his shirt.

His explanation was reasonable. She nodded. "Do you have magyck? If so, would you fix my hair?"

"Sure." Dallin ran a hand over her hair. "There you go." He indicated to a chair by the fire. "Why don't you sit down and eat something? We have a long journey ahead of us."

Lailii touched her hair, now soft and glossy from Dallin's magyck touch. She turned and stared at the two silver bars beside a goblet of wine. She smiled at Dallin and sat. Her hand trembled. How long had it been since she had eaten anything but stale bread, and now the idiot offered her a strange, metal bar? What cruel trick was this? Taking the unusual item between thumb and finger, she lifted her chin and sighed. "I'm sorry. I do not believe I can eat this."

"It's an energy bar." Dallin took the cookie from her hand and ripped open the foil wrapper. "They are from our time." He broke a little off the end of the bar and pushed it into his mouth. "Mmm, apple-cinnamon—my favorite. Take it slow. I don't want you to puke." He pressed a portion of the bar against Lailii's lips.

She took the morsel of crumbly delight and chewed slowly. Gods, it tasted so good. She reached for the goblet of wine and sipped. Dallin watched her with a puzzled expression.

She smiled at him. "I owe you my life. When my powers are restored, I will weave any spells of your choosing."

The door opened before Dallin could reply. Stryker strolled in with clothes hanging over his muscular arm. He stared at Lailii and smiled wickedly. "So you couldn't wait for me."

"We both need to bite her to ensure she transforms." Dallin shrugged. "My bite has healed her as the Lady promised."

"Yeah, I can see that." Stryker grinned at Lailii. "You are sure filling out kid."

Lailii's face grew hot. She glanced down. Dear Lady, her legs were exposed. She blinked. Her skinny legs had vanished and now appeared normal. In fact, her legs had never looked this good before. She pulled the sheet over her thighs.

"We're going to see you when you get dressed." Stryker balled his fists on his hips. "We are Pride; nudity comes with the territory. Hell, you'll be sharing our tent—get used to it."

In defiance, Lailii stood up and dropped the sheet. What the hell, they had already seen her naked. Gods, Dallin had washed her. Too late to be a prude now. She walked to Stryker and took the clothes from his arm. She forced an expression of indifference. "Well?"

"Outstanding." Stryker gave her a wide grin.

The man's gaze centered on her breasts. She glanced down. *Oh my, they are much bigger than I remembered.* With a toss of her hair, she held up a pair of buckskin breeches. "These are boy's clothes."

"That's all we could find." Stryker shrugged.

"Let her get dressed, and then we will bite her. With luck, she will transform overnight, and we can take her home." Dallin tipped his head toward the door. "You'll need to get Lance to wait with her while she finishes eating."

"Lance? Why can't *we* wait with her?"

"Because, he has a mate of his own at home and is the safest choice. After we bite her, I'll need to speak to you—in private." Dallin glared at his lover. "Go get Lance. Tell him to wait outside the door"

Dallin waited in silence until Stryker returned. He gave his friend a nod and turned to gaze at Lailii. Lady's blood, his cock ached for this female. His bite had replenished her emacited body, turning the child into a beautiful woman, ripe and ready for picking. Now he must bite her again. The entire episode was confusing and against tradition. Pride bite their mates—only their life mates—and now, by the Lady's command, he was sharing his venom with a wood nymph.

I guess the Lady knows what she is doing. I hope she factored in the fact, the female sends my cat into a frenzy. Gods, what if he lost control and raped her? The Lady would banish him to the Underworld.

Biting the inside of his cheek, Dallin searched his backpack for a tube of lube. *No doubt, she will affect Stryker the same way.* He pushed the tube into his pocket, turned to Lailii, and smiled. "The clothes will do for now. I will have the finest gowns made for you when we return to Demon Island."

"That place is a myth." Lailii pulled on a pair of boots and walked up and town, testing the fit. "It is mentioned in the Book of the Fae. Some say, fierce storms and tides protect Demon Island, and only the devil can gain entrance." She tossed her head. "I've heard many tales of the mythical Vane Warriors. They are told to frighten children."

Schooling his expression, Dallin moved closer to Stryker. "Interesting. You must tell me those stories around a campfire one night. Come here, little one."

"Are you going to bite me again now?" Lailii looked back and forth between Dallin and Stryker. "Won't you first please explain what you mean by transform?"

"We don't have time." Stryker met Lailii's gaze. "We must leave this place, or we will have to fight the entire Butcher's army. We have ten men with us; the Butcher will slaughter us. Do you want to go back to the dungeon?"

"No" Lailii stepped between the men and lifted her chin. "Please hurry."

Dallin bent his head and licked across his previous bite marks. He heard Stryker moan. Without waiting, they sank their fangs into Lailii's neck. His cat roared in pleasure. Lailii's scent hit Dallin like a train. Gods, he could smell her arousal. The bites were affecting her as well. She made small mews, and her nails dug deliciously into Dallin's back. He wanted her, right here, right now.

Drawing his fangs from her neck, Dallin met Stryker's hot gaze. The man turned his head away and called for Lance. Dallin helped Lailii to the chair by the fire and pressed a goblet of wine into her trembling hands. "Rest a while, and eat as much as you can. Lance will look after you while we are gone."

"I believe I need you close by." Lailii met Dallin's gaze. "I want you both to hold me. I have such strange feelings."

I want to crush those full lips and fill you with my aching cock. Soon, little one. "We will be back shortly, and then we will leave this dreadful place. You have my word. We will stay close for the journey back to Demon Island."

Dallin turned and marched from the room, indicating for Stryker to follow him. He hurried along the corridor and pushed open the next door. They rushed inside and shut the door. The room stunk of sweat and mildew. He couldn't care less. With a groan, he turned to Stryker and thrust him against the door, tearing at his lover's clothes. The man grasped his hair and dragged him into a long, hot kiss. Their tongues tangled. Dallin tasted the man's mouth, drinking in his familiar flavor mixed with the heady taste of venom and blood. He lifted his head on a sigh, and then nibbled a path down Stryker's neck. He pushed his hands under Stryker's tunic, seeking his lover's hot, silky flesh. "Pull down your pants; I have lube."

He pulled the lube from his pocket and squeezed some onto his fingertips, then handed the lube to Stryker. The man slowly replaced the lid and dropped the tube to the floor, his eyes smoldering.

Dallin growled. "Turn around."

With practiced ease, he lubed his cock and Stryker's star. The man bent over, his hands flat against the door panels, his golden ass a stark contrast to the room's dark wood walls. Dallin grasped his lover's hips and entered him in one long, delicious slide. He rode him hard, taking and giving pleasure. Grazing his fangs down Stryker's back, he moaned. "Do you like this? Tell me. Talk dirty to me."

"Gods, yes, you know I do. Fuck me harder . . . *ah* . . . make me come."

Dallin thrust his hips, riding the wave of intense pleasure. Stryker made the soft sound, the sign Dallin wanted to hear. His lover was near climax. He gave into the bliss, and they came together, crashing in a storm of delight. Not wanting the experience to end, Dallin slipped from his lover. Breathless, he turned Stryker around and drew him close, taking his mouth in a long, slow kiss. He raised his head. "Did you feel a powerful surge of lust mixed with a deep longing when we bit her?"

"Sure, it hit me like lightning." Stryker met Dallin's intense gaze. "Do you think she is 'the one'?"

"My cat sure thinks she is. He is going ballistic."

"Mine too." Stryker rubbed the back of his neck. "But we know nothing about her. I thought there would be some sort of courtship." He pulled up his pants. "You know, I think we should back off. We're here to do a job. The Lady would have told you if Lailii is our life mate."

Dallin took a packet of wipes from inside his shirt pocket and cleaned up. He shrugged. "She said that *you* were her other choice for me." He rubbed his chin. "If she meant as well as Lailii, it's easy enough to find out. Only our life mate will experience Moonfire from our venom, and only our chosen one can unlock our childseed." He grinned. "We'll take it one day at a time. I just thank the Lady you are here with me, or the Spellweaver would be on her back with her legs in the air right now."

Chapter Five

Lailii flexed her arms and smiled to herself. Her body looked and felt wonderful. She followed Dallin's broad back through the great hall. Every flagstone throughout the Butcher of Anwyn's castle showed signs of a bloody battle. "Did you kill everyone?"

"Yes. I couldn't leave a witness to inform the Butcher of our presence in your time. It was fortunate the Butcher left only a dozen men to guard the castle."

Dallin drew her against his armor. "The men we killed were mass murderers. It is well known they rape children, and they deserved their fate."

"You carry no sword, and yet the floors run red with blood."

"Do you remember the weapon I used to cut through the chains?" Dallin tapped a leather scabbard at his waist. "It's called a Zap. The magyck beam cuts through anything, even diamond, so I don't have to tell you what it does to a body." He squeezed Lailii. "My men have never fought an enemy with a sword. Moreover, we don't cut down men without provocation. My men sustained injuries, but most were from projectiles. The Butcher's men love to throw daggers."

They walked out into the courtyard. Lailii stepped away from Dallin, closed her eyes, and turned her face to the twin suns. She called to the Lady to replenish her powers. She opened her arms and spread her fingers, palms up. A surge of white light ignited her magyck and flowed through her body in comforting waves.

"Holy shit." Stryker stepped back. "Do you normally glow gold in the sun, sweetheart?"

"I've read about that phenomenon." Dallin stood his ground. "She is a Spellweaver; in ancient times they drew power from sunlight, moonlight and all the senses – including love." He chuckled. "Fuck, I bet she lights up for the right guy."

"No more sex with the light off then?" Stryker threw Dallin a mischievous grin. "Anything else I should know?"

"I'm guessing she has ancient magyck like plagues of locusts and the like." Dallin ran a hand through his hair. "Some of their curses held for generations."

Lailii put her hands on her hips and glared at the two men. "Would you mind not discussing me as if I'm not here? If you want to know something, ask me."

"So, is it true?" Stryker inclined his head. "What he said?"

"Yes."

"Cool." Stryker placed an arm around her shoulder. "If you ride with me, I'll help you regenerate your powers."

Slipping out from under his arm, Lailii smiled. *That would be very nice but I would like to know you better first.* "I have my own mount."

"There was only a donkey in the stable." Dallin frowned. "That poor old thing won't last a day in the desert."

With a smile, Lailii tipped her head back and called softly. "Argon."

She turned to Dallin. "My horse will come; can we please leave now? I need to be outside the castle grounds."

Dallin mounted Courage and held out his hand to Lailii. Pulling her across his thighs, he spurred his horse forward to lead his troops under the portcullis and across the drawbridge. His eyes widened. In the distance, a white horse approached. The warhorse thundered to a halt in a cloud of golden sand. His long, sparkling mane and tail flowed as if in slow motion. The magnificent beast reared high, pawed the air, and spun in a pirouette.

Lailii threw Dallin a grin, slid from his arms, and walked toward the beast. The horse pranced forward, every muscle quivering. Dallin held his breath. *The beast looks unbroken.* To his delight, Argon nuzzled Lailii's outstretched palm with his pink, velvet nose. The girl spoke softly to her mount, her small hand grasped a handful of mane, and she leapt with ease onto the stallion's back. Lailii rode toward him, grinning like a monkey. To his amazement, she controlled the beast without bridle or saddle. "Ride between me and Stryker at all times. We must cross the dunes. On the other side, my brother is waiting at the river with the rest of my troops."

"That is at least a twelve hour journey." Lailii moved her horse between the men. "We will need to rest the horses. Will we be making camp tonight?"

Dallin's cock pressed hard against the front of his pants. She would share their tent tonight. The sight of her full breasts and all that silky, platinum hair brushing her peach-colored skin would be hard to resist. He swallowed. "My main concern is getting over the first dune and out of sight. The Butcher won't be too happy when he returns tonight to find his men are dead. I'm guessing he will be hot on our trail." He met her silver gaze. "The air is still. Our prints will be in the sand, making an easy trail for any numbskull to follow."

"Do I *really* belong to you now, Prince Dallin?" Lailii tossed her long hair over one shoulder.

"Yes, you belong to me and Stryker."

"Then I will weave spells on your command. I will protect you to the best of my ability."

"We have magyck. Each of us has a special talent. Dallin has the ability to cloak, to become invisible, and I am a Dream walker." Stryker snorted and shot her a glance. "What can *you* actually do?"

"I can weave any spell you require." She giggled. "I can command the wind to wipe away our tracks. Tonight, if you wish to cook or stay warm, I can conjure a black fire, which produces no smoke or light."

"That will be very useful. Can you build an invisible force field around your body as a defense?" Stryker shot Dallin a glance. "Or jump from one place to the other?"

"No." Lailii frowned. "I assume when you say 'jump' you are referring to something other than bouncing on one's feet?"

Dallin touched her hand. "We can move short distances instantaneously."

"If you can form a protective barrier around your bodies, how did your men get injured during battle?" Lailii curled her fingers around Dallin's hand.

Without thinking, he squeezed her small fingers. Her touch thrilled him. He pulled his hand away and cleared his throat. "Unfortunately, you can't fight through a barrier or discharge a weapon; it would bounce back."

"I have much to learn about your time. Will you teach me your magycks and any other things you deem necessary, so I may please you both, my lord?"

Dallin grinned. *Oh, sweetheart, you're killing me.* "Don't worry; we will teach you *everything* you need to know."

* * * * *

The twin suns had reached the highest point in the sky by the time Lailii and her rescuers climbed the crest of the first sand dune. Lailii looked down the other side to the shifting, crimson sands shimmering in the midday heat. On this side of the desert, desolate sand in every shade of red spread out in an endless carpet of dunes to the horizon. Grit filled her mouth, and sand clung to her sweat-soaked skin. She turned to Dallin. "Shall I obliterate our tracks now, sir?"

"Yes, thank you, and please, little one, my name is Dallin."

Argos danced on the spot, his tail flashing from side to side. Lailii waited until the troops filed down the other side of the dune. She turned Argos to the west, and then opened her arms and summoned the wind. At first, a light breeze brushed her hot skin. Far in the distance, the wind roared. The twin suns darkened, hidden behind a wall of sand. The magyck storm whipped up the desert floor, forming a line of golden vortexes. They grew stronger and danced across the sand in mini tornadoes, swirling away any traces of their journey. At a clap of her hands, the wind dropped, and the oppressive heat returned.

"Well done." Dallin pressed a canteen into her hand. "Stryker will draw water from the sand for the horses. We will rest for half an hour. I plan to reach the oasis before nightfall."

Dallin watched her drink. His gaze settled on her lips. Hell, he wanted to lap at the drop of water spilling from the corner of her mouth. *My cock is so hard . . . another hour in the saddle and I'll be a eunuch.* He groaned. Lust burned his balls with each swipe of her pink tongue across her full, delicious lips. Why did he feel this way? *Look at her; her face is streaked with dirt, her hair crusted with sand.* The untidy image should put a man off—but not him, hell no. He wanted to throw her down on the sand to fuck her long and slow, right now.

One of his men, Brad, came over to take his horse to the water hole. He glared at the man and stood in front of Lailii. The thought of any male looking at her heated his blood. Dallin turned to draw her close to his side. His cat purred. *I like her too, cat.*

"*Mine*"

* * * * *

Late that afternoon, they climbed to the top of another sand dune. In the distance, the twin suns hovered above the horizon. Stryker breathed a sigh of relief. Toward the east, an oasis broke the red sand with a welcoming, green splash of color. They had stashed supplies in a cave there for the return journey. He smiled at the thought of a bath, clean clothes, and a hot meal. Gods, he hated the desert.

He glanced at Dallin. The man insisted he stay beside him the entire journey, which suited Stryker just fine. The need to stay close to Lailii overpowered him. She drew him like a magnet. Never before had he felt the need to touch a woman so often. He liked the way she giggled; his heart raced at her smile. One accidental brush of her hand and he grew rock hard. *I wonder if Dallin is feeling the same. What do you say, cat?*

"*Mine.*"

Somehow, I thought you'd say that. We have to wait; be patient, and don't push me. Trust me, buddy, I want her too.

Within the hour, they reached the oasis. Dallin's men rushed around collecting tents and supplies from the cave. Lailii slid off Argos and allowed the horse to forage for food. She walked to the edge of the lagoon and gazed at the surrounding dense foliage and palm trees heavy with fruit. A flock of noisy parrots gathered at the water's edge, drinking their fill, oblivious to the men erecting tents. Lailii took a deep breath of the clean air and sighed. *A few hours ago, I thought I would die in that rat-infested dungeon. Thank the Lady that Dallin rescued me.*

Although she heard no sound, she knew Dallin and Stryker were behind her. She turned and smiled at them. They were so handsome, and her heart fluttered every time they came close. "This is a beautiful place."

"There is a secluded area, a bit farther along, where you can swim." Stryker took Lailii's hand and led her along an overgrown pathway. "We can *fresh and clean* our clothes for tomorrow, but I thought you may like to wear one of my spare tunics tonight."

Lailii glanced back at Dallin. The man looked fierce. "That would be nice, thank you. Is 'fresh and clean' a spell?"

"Yes." Dallin took her other hand. "Our tent will be some distance from my troops. I must ask you not to wander away from our tent." He squeezed Lailii's hand. "Will you show me the spell for black fire? I'm sure my men would enjoy a hot meal tonight."

With grin, Lailii stopped and looked at the two huge men. "I can light a stick and you can pass it on to your men for the fires. I think teaching is best when we are safely away from the Butcher."

"We learn very fast, little one." Dallin shrugged. "I understand you may be reluctant to share your spells, but I can assure you, in my time, everyone uses magyck."

At the bottom of a huge rock formation, the men had finished erecting a large tent. Surrounded on one side by palm trees and in the shade of the rock, it made an ideal camp. Lailii glanced inside the tent. In the center stood a table set with goblets and plates. She noticed a fat wine skin hanging from a hook on the center pole. Then her gaze fell on the bed. Not a hard pallet but a large, soft construction covered with white sheets. *One bed for the three of us – oh my stars.*

"Will you make the black fire now?" Dallin handed her a dead branch. "Then we can wash off this damn sand."

Gathering her magyck, Lailii concentrated on the stick. A black flame burst into life at the tip; the wood crackled under the intense heat. She held out the stick to Dallin. The Pride took the stick, handed it to one of his men, and rattled off a string of orders. Lailii turned to him. "Is it customary for males to sleep together in your time?"

"If they are lovers." Dallin took her hand and led her toward the lagoon. "And to answer your next question, Stryker and I like girls too."

"Does the fact that we have sex together upset you?" Stryker took her other hand.

It is a most simulating thought. "No."

"Tell us about yourself; where do you come from?" Dallin stopped in a small clearing. "How did the Butcher capture you and why?"

Lailii stood motionless and watched the two men undress. Dallin gave her a confident smile and began undoing her shirt. She slapped his hands away. "I can undress myself."

She disrobed slowly. Both men were aroused and watching her every move. The sight of their massive cocks would remain in her mind forever. Clearing her throat, Lailii set her gaze on a nearby rock. "I don't remember my family. They sent me to the Tark at the age of two summers." She pulled off her boots. "There, I studied to become a Spellweaver. Prince Derik bought me, and I served him for two years." Lailii slid off her buckskin pants and stood naked before the men. "The prince was taking his bride to Mulway. The Butcher attacked the Prince, and I remained behind, holding a spell until my prince rode to safety."

"He made no attempt to rescue you?" Stryker strode into the water.

"Obviously not— the bastard." Dallin followed Stryker into the lagoon and dived under the water.

The cool water looked so inviting. Lailii chewed on her bottom lip and stepped into the shallows. "The Butcher said he would hold me until Passio arrived and that I would be of value to the lord of the Underworld."

Stryker moaned. Gods, the female had a body to die for—an amazing ass, and great tits with hard, erect nipples. He could almost taste the succulent buds in his mouth. Her naturally hairless, peach-fuzz pussy would weep under his tongue. Shooting a glance at Dallin, he reached for Lailii's hand and dragged her under the water. She rose spluttering, her platinum hair stuck to her cheeks. He drew her against his body, her hot flesh pressed against him, and his cat went on full alert. "Sorry, sweetheart, I just wanna get you clean."

"I have to ask, little one." Dallin swam to her side. "Did the Butcher or his men rape you? Could you be pregnant?"

"No. They were too afraid." She grinned. "I cursed them. If one should rape me then his cock would go black and fall off."

Allowing his hands to roam over Lailii's soft skin, Stryker nuzzled her neck. "We will never rape you." He kissed her cheek. "I hope you will let us both love you."

"I know nothing of lovemaking, although your caresses are soothing." She turned in Stryker's arms. "I am a maiden."

"Well, then, we had better get you back to camp." Dallin splashed from the water. "It will be dark soon."

"Is he angry with me?" Lailii met Stryker's gaze.

Stryker laughed. He pulled her close and nuzzled her ear. "No. It's just that you being a virgin puts a whole new light on things. Come on, I'm starving. Let's go and see what's for dinner."

* * * * *

The twin suns set rapidly in the desert. Less than a second after they hit the horizon, the world became dark. In the black velvet sky, a crescent moon gave little light to show the way back to the tent, but the stars shone like a thousand diamonds. Dressed in Stryker's tunic, she followed him through the dense bushes. As they walked, Lailii turned to look at Stryker and clasped a hand over her mouth. Lady's blood, the man's eyes glowed in the dark. Fear cramped her legs, and she stumbled. Stryker's strong hands caught her with ease.

"You're trembling; what's the matter?" Stryker drew her close. "Does the darkness remind you of the dungeon?"

No, but you remind me of a demon. "Your eyes startled me. They glow."

95

"I'm a cat." Stryker shrugged. "We are shifters. We are both man and cat. I can see in the dark and so will you when you transform."

Lailii swallowed hard. What had she done? "I am going to become a *cat*?"

"You will be Pride, both female and cat." Stryker took hold of both of her hands, his thumbs making soothing circles. "It is nothing to fear. Transformation enhances sight, hearing, and stamina. After you produce your first cub, you will be able to morph into a cat and hunt."

"C-cub?" Lailii tried to pull away, but Stryker held her fast. "I'm not sure if I can feed a cat at my breast."

"Lailii—sweetness, look at me." Stryker grinned. "Our females do not give birth to *cats*. Our cubs are flesh and the same as us. We refer to our babes as *cubs*."

Meeting his glowing gaze in the darkness, Lailii drew a deep breath. The scent of Stryker wafted over her, bringing a wave of incredible calm. She nodded. "That's a relief."

They continued along the pathway and entered the tent. Soft, floating, magyck light globes cast a milky brightness to each corner. The aroma of a spicy meat dish filled the air. Lailii's stomach rumbled. Inside the tent, Dallin waved her to a seat, and then pressed a goblet of aromatic wine into her hand. She smiled up at him and sipped the wine. Her taste buds exploded with a melody of flavors. She swirled the wine around her mouth and moaned with delight.

"Ah, so you like Miza." Dallin chuckled. "Some call it Devil's Blood. It is a favorite of all Pride and Fae."

The men sat each side of her and began to offer her small portions of food from their plates. "Thank you, but I can feed myself."

"This is the way Pride males care for their females." Stryker lifted a honeyed pear to Lailii's lips. "We will take care of all your needs. From now on, you may not take food from any other."

Before Lailii could lick her lips, Stryker bent forward and lapped at the sticky juice dripping down her chin. The simple move sent erotic shivers straight to her pussy. She met his sultry gaze, and the unfamiliar wetness between her legs returned. As they brushed against her to offer more food, her breasts grew heavy, and her nipples tingled. *I am acting like a wanton.* Fighting to draw the next breath, she turned to accept a portion of fruit from Dallin. "Why?"

"It is what we do, little one." He shrugged. "Life mates are treated with respect and love."

Lailii looked from one to the other. *Impossible, a prince deserves more than a mere Spellweaver. I am far too insignificant for these mighty warriors.* "You—both of you—want me for a life mate?"

"We have no choice in the matter; the Lady chooses our mates." Stryker wiped another piece of succulent pear across her lips. "Although, we both agree you would be an excellent choice." He smiled. "When you transform, if you belong to us, you will enter Moonfire. It is a time when females have an insatiable sex drive. A life mate's venom triggers Moonfire.

"Normally, a male only bites his life mate. In your case, the Lady Herself ordered us to bite you." Stryker rubbed his chin. "Although both our cats insist you belong to us, we will have to wait and see."

The possibility of both men bedding her ran through her mind. She remembered the short talk on *wifely duties* from the witch at the Tark. How could she possibly accommodate two men? Her face grew hot. *Gods, look at them; they really mean what they say.* Gathering her courage, she drew a deep breath. "As I said before, I'm not experienced, but from what I *do* know, females are made for *one* mate *not* two."

"We have shared many females, little one." Dallin stroked Lailii's cheek. "I promise, females can take two men and enjoy the experience immensely."

Oh my. "May I think on this proposition for a while?"

"Of course you can." Stryker refilled her goblet. "We would never force you to do anything."

"You must drink the Miza, little one." Dallin winked. "Then, we'll leave you to sleep in peace."

Lailii drank down the rich wine and allowed Stryker to refill her glass. The wine filled her head with a comforting drowsiness. "Will you be here when I wake up?"

"I can assure you, we will be by your side." Dallin got to his feet.

She watched the men leave the tent, emptied her goblet, and got unsteadily to her feet. Taking a few wobbly steps, she fell onto the soft bed. She stared at the patterns dancing across the canvas. Her face grew hot with erotic thoughts of the two, perfect males planning to share her bed.

Chapter Six

Dreams surged through Lailii's sleep. *The dreamscape became vivid and filled with rich colors. No longer human, she had sleek, white fur with stripes of black. Her vision grew sharp; the bright images were almost painful. She lifted her head and gazed up into the canopy of a lush rainforest. Thousands of trees rose high above, their branches laden with twisted vines. Lailii dropped her gaze. Below, in the rich, brown earth, an endless procession of ants carried a dead butterfly held high above their tiny* bodies. *She turned and bounded with ease over thick roots in a tangle of gnarled, witch's fingers. Running between the trees, she inhaled the scents of the forest, and then stopped to brush her face in the wild orchids, wet with dew. Leaping through clumps of fragrant wild flowers, she snapped her teeth at the clouds of butterflies. Monkeys chatted nervously above, swinging from tree to tree, alerting the wildlife to her presence. Birds fled their roosts, soaring through the branches in noisy bursts of color. She purred. The monkeys were safe – today, she hunted for a mate.*

In the distance, Lailii heard the sound of trickling water and moved closer. She hesitated before a water hole bathed in leopard spots of sunlight and raised her head to sniff the air. She scented the presence of two males. Her heart raced. Turning her head from side to side, she searched the velvet shade.

On the perimeter of the clearing, concealed within the zebra shadows, stood two magnificent males. A powerful, white tiger moved into plain sight and purred his welcome. A silver Lynx followed and lowered his massive head. Lailii knew these cats by scent alone – her life mates.

Lailii's nipples ached and her pussy tingled with an unfamiliar desire. She moaned and opened her eyes. Inside the tent, darkness closed around her like a shroud. She turned her head and recognized Dallin's unique scent on one side and Stryker's masculine musk on the other. Dallin's warm hand ran down her thigh; his casual stroke electrified her. She wanted his touch and fought the desire to nuzzle against his naked body. *What in the Lady's name is happening to me?*

Erotic desire flamed so hot, Lailii's skin burned. She sat up and tore at the tunic. She whipped it off over her head and flung the damp material to the floor. Dallin's large hand skimmed down her back. The simple gesture soaked her pussy. Gods, her thighs were wet with the evidence of her desire. Overwhelmed with passion, Lailii rubbed her cheek along Stryker's back, and then crawled onto Dallin's hard, muscular body. She bent her head and licked his chest, her tongue lapping at his flat nipples. His unique scent flooded her mouth; her womb clenched. *I don't know what to do.*

"Little one." Dallin drew her tight against him. "Do you need me?"

Not able to answer, Lailii pressed her mouth against his warm, sensual lips. Dallin moved against her in a slow, sensual rhythm. His hot tongue pressed against her teeth, demanding entrance. So exquisite, the way his tongue caressed every part of her mouth . . . she kissed him back, meeting him stroke for stroke. His long fingers slid into her pussy, and he sighed into her mouth. When he removed his tantalizing fingers, she moaned and arched her back to rub her aching breasts against his damp chest. She needed more.

"You must tell me that you want me, little one." Dallin pushed the hair from Lailii's face. "I will not take a virgin in an act of lust." He ran both hands down her arms. "Do you recognize me as your life mate?"

Lailii met his gaze. In the darkness, she could see his eyes glowing. "I see you and Stryker in my dreams as cats. I want both of you. I *need* both of you. Please don't make me choose."

"Only one may be your first; I will be honored if it's me." Dallin kissed Lailii's neck.

"That's not really true." Stryker yawned. "I can have her virginity in other ways." He pushed up on one elbow. "Does this mean she has transformed? Holy cow, she smells good enough to eat. This must be her Moonfire."

"Oh, yes . . . and she has the most delightful fangs." Dallin chuckled. "Gods, she is so hot and wet." He lifted Lailii off his chest and placed her on her back beside Stryker.

"I didn't believe my cat. He insisted she belonged to us." Stryker grinned into the darkness. "This is absolute proof."

I'm not beautiful; why would they want me? White, hot, erotic surges pulsed along Lailii's thighs and shot deep inside her pussy. Her doubts vanished with each trembling shudder. She gripped Dallin's massive forearm. "Please, I can't stand this . . . I need . . . please—you must both take me." Lailii met Stryker's gaze. "You said it was possible. If so . . . I choose both of you."

"The first time will hurt, little one." Dallin stroked her breast. "After, there will pleasure. I promise."

Both men rolled onto their sides and captured Lailii's nipples in their hot mouths. She cried out, the sensation so wonderful, so intense. Her fingers entwined in their silky hair; she arched her back, offering more to her lovers. Dallin took her face between his large hands and kissed her. His deep, passionate kiss possessed and demanded. The man's long hair brushed her nipples in a soft caress. Hot, sensual fire licked across her body, creating marvelous waves of desire. She squirmed on the bed, wanting so much more.

Stryker mumbled under his breath and pressed damp kisses down her belly. Lailii gasped. His mouth had reached her apex. His probing tongue slipped inside her soaked folds and swirled around. She opened her legs at his insistence, then lifted her hips to get more of him. Tingling sensations, wonderful, frightening throbs of delicious pleasure filled her pussy. This must be wrong. The witch at the Tark mentioned nothing about this delightful sex play. *Dear Lady, will I die from such pleasure?*

Without warning, Stryker rolled away. She cried out in frustration. Stryker's long fingers replaced his tongue and circled the pleasure point. His wet mouth closed over her nipple and suckled.

"We'll make this so good for you." Dallin rolled on top of her. "Lift up your knees for me."

Dallin held her hips and rested the tip of his cock against her soaking pussy. She bucked at the intimate contact, her eyes wide. The female was so close to climax, and Stryker would make sure she came the moment he entered her. The man was a genius. Dallin bit his bottom lip. He must take it slow or ruin their life mate. His balls ached with the urge to plunge in and ride her hard. His cat screamed in his head.

Lailii's hot pussy quivered against Dallin's cock. Her silky-smooth legs trembled. He thrust his hips and slid into paradise. Her tight channel clamped around his shaft in glorious waves of heat. One more thrust and he tore her barrier. Her mouth opened in a silent scream. He gathered her against him and kissed her. When he met her gaze again, her eyes were deep pools of passion. Without hesitation, he moved inside her, in long, smooth, strokes until her channel pulsed around his cock.

Lailii tried to focus. The twin suns had begun to rise, and the interior of the tent became a kaleidoscope of brilliance. Dallin rolled with her until she straddled his hips. His massive shaft buried deep inside her, sending wonderful sensations with every thrust. He pulled her close to his damp body and reined kisses over her face. The man's hot gaze hid nothing of his pleasure.

Behind her, Stryker caressed her back, her buttocks, and then applied a cool balm to her ass. His finger dipped inside, and her face grew hot from the forbidden delight. *Why does he stroke my ass?*

"Relax, little one, and the pain will be over in a few seconds." Dallin nibbled her ear. "Don't fight the pain, relax."

Pain? I think I'm enjoying the touch of those fingers too much. With a sigh, Lailii rested her head on Dallin's shoulder. In the early morning light, the vein in his throat throbbed before her eyes. Drawn to taste his skin once more, she licked and then dragged her fangs across his jugular. She inhaled his intoxicating scent. Her face ached, the need to bury her fangs deep in his neck, overpowering. She ran her tongue over her teeth. *Gods, I can't believe I have fangs.*

The heat of Stryker's body pressed against her. His kisses teased her back. The moment his hot cock pressed against her forbidden hole, the act of taking two men at once slammed home. She opened her mouth to protest, but Stryker entered her in one quick thrust. Sharp pain exploded inside her. Stryker's hot shaft stretched her to the limit. She screamed and buried her fangs deep in Dallin's throat.

So full, Lailii moaned at the delicious, twin sensations of two men thrusting deep inside. The pain vanished into hot waves of delight. Dallin's sweet blood filled her mouth. She bit deeper, her cheeks pumped, and the pain in her face subsided. Strange visions filled her mind, of running through the forest as a tiger or flying through the air on a strange contraption. She experienced Dallin's deep love for his family and Stryker. The man's intense desire for her warmed her heart. *Lady's blood, I can see into the man's soul.*

Pinned between her lovers' damp bodies, Lailii withdrew her fangs. The scents of her mates poured over her. She inhaled, drawing the rich, potent, male musk deep into her lungs. Nothing should feel this good. Every nerve in her body screamed with the intensity of her mates' thrusts. She gasped their names, gave in to the searing, endless passion, and shuddered to a violent climax. As if by silent agreement, both men followed, filling her with incredible, liquid heat. They clung together, both men dragging in ragged breaths.

"Thank the Lady, the darling bit me." Dallin ran a hand over his face. "You must take her again. She must bite you as well."

Stryker slipped from her and went to pour water into a bowl to wash. His knees trembled. So much emotion welled inside him; tears pricked the backs of his eyes. He had waited for this moment all his adult life. Lady's blood, they had found their mate.

"It is not possible to perform again so soon— even a stallion needs to rest after coupling." Lailii rested her head on Dallin's chest. "You surely jest."

"We are Pride, little one." Dallin rolled her onto her back and slipped from her. "We are insatiable and can make love frequently, in fact, whenever we desire."

With a grin, Stryker moved closer to the bed. "Although, we both understand the tenderness of a virgin and will make allowances. Let me see if I can make you come again, sweet thing."

In the gray, early morning light, Lailii's damp body gave off a subtle, golden glow. Stryker grinned. *So, it is true; she does light up for the right men.* "You are so very beautiful."

"Not many would agree with you." Lailii glanced away.

"Put aside any bad memories, little one. You have a new life with us." Dallin sat on the side of the bed. "Just enjoy."

Stryker took her into his arms. Such a small female for two warriors, Lailii's elfin features entranced him. He kissed the side of her mouth and licked a trail across her bottom lip. Her full breasts pressed against his chest, the rosy nipples hard and begging him to suck them. He would savor this moment, this taking of his life mate. He inhaled her perfect, feminine scent and knew his cat rolled with delight. Lailii wet her succulent lips and lifted her head, seeking his mouth. Stryker growled, bent his head, and kissed her hard—she tasted like sin. He cupped her breast, circling her nipple with the pad of his thumb.

She arched, pushing her tight bud into his hand. Beside him, Dallin caressed Lailii's clit, his face forming a mask of concentration. Stryker lifted his head and gazed into the man's eyes—cat's eyes. He knew his would be the same. His cat crawled close to the surface, vying for control. The need to mate Lailii rushed though his loins, and blood pounded in his ears. The Spellweaver undulated beneath him. Her long, sharp nails raked his back.

"Take me." Lailii rubbed against Stryker. "My face aches; I need to bite you."

She opened for him, and her slim legs wrapped around his waist. Stryker entered her with care. So damn tight, he could barely move. Her slick channel gripped him in her heat. Lailii's mews of encouragement drove him forward. He plunged deep and rode her in short thrusts. She bit like a snake, fast and deep. Her venom rushed through his veins in molten lust. Their minds joined, and he knew the pain she had suffered in the dungeon. Saw her self-doubt, and the deep loneliness she had endured her entire life.

Stryker lowered his body, drawing her closer, letting her drink her fill. She lifted her head, her lips stained crimson with his blood. No other female had ever looked so beautiful. *My mate.*

"I need you too." Dallin moved behind Stryker.

The cool swipe of lube swept across his ass, and then Dallin entered him in one hard, sizzling thrust. Stryker groaned. The exquisite sensation each time Dallin brushed his pleasure spot, mixed with the tight, hot wetness of Lailii's pussy, shattered his control. He bucked his hips, meeting Dallin's deep thrusts. Under his chest, Lailii giggled, her silver eyes dancing with delight. Stryker drove into her wetness.

The female's tight pussy began to pulsate around him. He trembled, reveling in the incredible sensations. His cock grew hot, and his balls tightened. White spots danced before his eyes. His lover gave one hard shove and filled him, shouting his climax. The man's delicious heat tipped Stryker over the edge. With a roar of triumph, he came in long, shuddering gushes.

* * * * *

Later that morning, as the twin suns climbed to the highest point in the sky, they reached the top of the last dune. Sand crusted Lailii's wet lips. All morning, they had trailed in the dust of the troops, her mates insisting on her remaining downwind. The enticing scent of her Moonfire had set the entire camp of randy cats on edge.

Lailii could see the edge of the desert merging into green fields. A fast-flowing, azure river wound away in the distance, disappearing into a lush, emerald forest. She knew this place; Prince Derik's castle rested to the north at the foot of the Mulway Mountain. Her stomach clenched. What would happen if they met the prince? Would he demand that she return to him?

"What is wrong, little one?" Dallin moved Courage closer to Argos.

She met his swirling amethyst gaze. "Prince Derik lives to the north of here. He often hunts in the forest." She swallowed hard. "If we meet him, he will expect me to return to Mulway Castle with him."

"I hope we do meet him." Dallin snorted. "There are a few choice words I have to say to the wimp."

"You belong to us." Stryker leaned toward Lailii and touched her face. "We will kill anyone who thinks different."

Lailii pulled on Argos' mane to stop him. She glared at Stryker in disbelief. "Kill Prince Derik? I am sworn to protect him with my life."

"All bets were off when he deserted you, sweetheart." Stryker frowned. "I will tear him to pieces with my bare hands for what he did to you. Don't you dare try to defend the pig. You *belong* to us now, not that asshole."

With a sob, Lailii looked from one angry face to the other. "Do you believe I would *want* to go back to a man who deems me no more than an insignificant slave?" She rubbed her fists into her eyes. "Well, I don't, but I gave my sacred oath to serve him."

"The Lady gave you into our protection. She spoke to me." Dallin took Lailii's face in his hand. "You are our life mate. No oath to any male comes before *our* sacred bond."

The warm fragrance of her mates surrounded her; gods, they exuded their scent at will. She drank it in, allowing the calming effect to sooth her nerves. Her pussy creamed. She ached for them. She met Dallin's hot gaze. "I know in my heart this is true."

"I know you burn for us, little one." Dallin brushed his thumb across Lailii's bottom lip. "Moonfire is cruel when we can't be alone with you.

It's not much farther to the camp. We will remain there for a couple of days. Then we will take you home."

Cruel? They had no idea. Lailii reached for Dallin's canteen and sipped the cool water. With each small movement, her nipples, tender from lovemaking, rubbed against the harsh fabric of her shirt, driving her to madness. She could still feel her lover's mouths suckling on the sensitive tips and the touch of their damp skin sliding across her flesh. With her legs stretched across Argos' back and her soaking pussy wide open, each step sent white-hot shimmers cascading from her swollen clit. Gods, her body tingled from their intimate touch, and her womb clenched each time her gaze fell to their cocks. Beneath their tight pants, the outline of smooth, velvet skin stretched over steel made her mouth water. They wanted her even after a night of love. She could see their arousal — arousal for her.

Cheers greeted their arrival at the river. Lailii could count at least twenty troops. The camp sprawled along the riverbank. Dallin put on his warrior face, took his canteen from Lailii's hands, and left her under the shade of a weeping willow. She turned and smiled at Stryker. "I wish I could dive into the river; it looks so cool."

"Soon." He moved his horse closer to her mount. "Your scent will send the men into a frenzy if we are not careful. Dallin will make sure our tent is erected in a safe place."

Lailii pulled a face. "Must I go through life afraid a Pride will rape me?"

"Come here, sweetheart." Stryker lifted Lailii from the back of her horse and draped her across his thighs. "Pride males do not rape. During Moonfire, the female's scent is strong. Without a female to comfort them, the males become restless and fight a lot. The need for constant sex is part of being a Pride male."

Stryker held her close and inhaled her fragrance. His cock pressed hard against the front of his pants. His cat purred contentedly. *His woman, his mate.* He smiled and rested his chin on the top of her head. This small, elfin female had taken them both all night. Her moans of delight had told him she enjoyed their lovemaking. Her small body had opened for them, and she had given them both more than they could ever need. She nestled closer. Her long, platinum hair brushed the skin on his arm, and this slight caress sent a surge of lust straight to his balls.

Gods, he could still taste her pussy and wanted to feast again on her silky smooth petals. Then drive into her until she cried out his name in passion. With a groan, he nuzzled her neck. His face ached to bite her again. She responded and turned her sweet face up to him, her mouth seeking his. Lost in the kiss, he held her close until Dallin's voice broke the spell.

"I have posted guards around our tent. All of them trusted men, with their own life mates. We need to hunt. Cruz mentioned a herd of deer grazing not a hundred feet away in the forest." Dallin smiled at

Lailii. "You may bathe in the rock pool in peace, little one."

"Thank you." Lailii smiled. "I'm hungry too."

Stryker slipped his hand under Lailii's shirt and cupped her breast. She moaned and pressed the hard nipple into his palm. "Relax in the pool, and we'll feed you when we return." He met her sultry gaze. "I want you nice and relaxed, sweetness, so we can fuck you all night long."

"Oh . . . yeah." Dallin pushed his mount closer and ran a hand down Lailii's thigh. "Tell me you want us, little one."

"I want you." Lailii squirmed under their touch. "I have thought of nothing else all day."

"Oh, sweetheart." Stryker lifted her shirt to expose her full, white mounds. He bent his head and licked one taut, rosy nipple.

"If you keep that up, we won't be hunting tonight." Dallin shot Stryker an angry gaze. "My cat needs to hunt—let's go."

Dallin dismounted and led the way to the tent. He lifted Lailii from Stryker's horse and set her on her feet. He pointed to a secluded rock pool surrounded with trees. "I have left a towel and a clean tunic by the pool. My men are a discrete distance away. No one will come near you. We will be in the forest for about an hour. Can you wait that long before you eat?"

"Yes, a long soak will ease the cramps from riding." She smiled up at him. "I'll be fine; my magyck will protect me."

Like it protected you from the Butcher of Anwyn? Lady's blood, you have no idea what a demon might do to you. "Go and take a bath. Don't worry; my men would die to protect you."

Lailii shot him a mischievous grin and walked toward the rock pool. Gods, he loved the way her hips swayed. Her small, peach-shaped bottom fit perfectly in the palms of his hands. He ached to take her tight little ass. He groaned. *Tonight, sweet thing.*

"Fuck, she is like a wet dream." Stryker cupped his balls. "I can't stop wanting to sink my cock into her hot little pussy."

Dallin raised a brow. "I'm betting my father will be disappointed. He wanted me to take a Si-Rani female. He told me the Oracle had foretold the joining of the Prides the day I was born."

"She is the Lady's choice." Stryker snorted. "Like he can say anything now she has bitten us."

"You know my father. He can *make* things happen his way."

"You have enough gold to live five lifetimes." Stryker shrugged. "If he wants to cause a problem, we'll go and live in another realm. One thing is for certain, we're not giving her up."

"He would have to kill me first." Dallin met Stryker's green gaze. "Trust me, that ain't gonna happen."

* * * * *

Lailii glanced around the rock pool. If Dallin's men were close, they had concealed themselves out of her sight. She lifted her chin to inhale the damp air, her skin tingling with the beauty of the place. Her body glowed, drawing power from every direction. The river, a wide, glistening expanse, fed from a massive waterfall, tumbled over rocks, sending rainbow sprays in every direction. Whitewater bubbled into the pool, highlighting the myriad of colors in the multifaceted rocks.

Lizards lazed in the sunshine, their eyes closed, their skin changing color from bright yellow to green at each passing cloud. Along the river's edge, deer bent their soft, chestnut heads to drink. Lailii swallowed. *Soon, I will hunt those beautiful creatures. I will have a cat to share my soul. I feel it bumping against my conscience, trying to emerge.*

Pushing her thoughts away, she undressed and eased her hot body into the cool water. She lay back and relaxed, dozing in the sunlight. The bubbles danced across her skin in a lover's caress. She moaned and turned her body back and forth, enjoying the erotic sensations. Her mates had made her wanton. She smiled. *I'm sure there is so much more. I need to taste their long, velvet cocks. The desire is becoming an obsession. Will they accept my mouth on them?*

Sometime later, a flash of color and a splash brought a man beside her. He rose from the water, flicking a mass of long, black hair over his broad, golden shoulder. His handsome face was familiar, so like Dallin he could almost be his twin. She drew her magyck around her, ready to fight. Heart pounding, Lailii covered her breasts and pressed her back against a rock.

"Don't be afraid, babe." The man gazed down at her. "I had no idea wood nymphs roamed this forest."

He stood over her, so huge his body blocked out the sun. Water droplets streamed down his naked body. Lailii blinked. This must be Dallin's brother. She allowed her magyck to recede. "I-I . . . I am a Spellweaver."

Roars broke the silence, sending birds screaming into the air. The lizards fled into the safety of the rocks. Lailii glanced away from the man to see two blood-covered, white cats plunging into the rock pool. A wave of water crashed over her head, dragging her into a swirling torrent. A forearm closed around her waist, pulling her back, pressed hard against a wall of hot muscle. She spluttered, gasped for air, and stared into her mates' faces. Both men's eyes glowed amber with rage.

"I find a sweet wood nymph to warm my bed, and you try to drown her." The man nuzzled her neck. "If you apologize, brother, I may let you have her tomorrow."

Stryker trembled with rage. His cat rose to the surface, ready to fight to the death for its mate. He ground his teeth and pushed down his cat. Dallin must speak to his brother. He shot a glance at his lover. The man fisted his hands at his sides.

"Let her go, Cruz." Dallin stared at his brother. "She is the Spellweaver we rescued."

"She mentioned that she was a Spellweaver." Cruz cupped Lailii's breast, his thumb making lazy circles around the nipple. "I'm happy to share."

With a growl, Stryker splashed forward and dragged Lailii into his arms. "She belongs to us."

"Don't tangle with me, little cat." Cruz growled. "You're no match for an alpha."

"Lailii is our life mate." Dallin stepped forward. "You must be blind not to notice that she carries our marks."

"You let the little minx bite you?" Cruz grinned. "Gods, father *will* be pleased."

"I'll expect you to honor my choice." Dallin stepped to one side. "Lailii, this is my brother, Cruz."

"He is the heir, and *I* am one of the spares, sweet lady." Cruz inclined his head. "Her scent is making me hard. You'll need to keep her away from the troops."

"No, *you* will need to keep them away." Dallin glared at Cruz. "We need two days to complete the mating."

"Sure . . . but you'll owe me." Cruz grinned.

Stryker covered Lailii with his arms. She pressed her small body against him. Her acceptance of his protection warmed his heart. Beneath his hands, her heart pounded; her long hair pressed against his hard shaft. He growled at Cruz. "Leave us and go check the guards are in place."

"Do you expect me to take orders from your lover?" Cruz shot a glance at Dallin.

"Moonfire makes us a little crazy." Dallin shrugged. "The need to protect our mate supersedes common courtesy." He laid a hand on his brother's shoulder. "Stryker knows the Butcher could have Gates we are unaware of, and that he may arrive at any moment. We could be at risk of attack."

"Don't tell me there could have been an easier way to rescue the girl? Fuck, why didn't you ask the Lady?" Cruz pushed wet hair off his face.

"The Lady gave me little information about this realm." Dallin turned to Lailii. "Do you know of travel Gates the Butcher could have used?"

"I know demons have the power to open travel fissures, not unlike our Gates. It is conceivable that the Butcher has many of these at his disposal. When he attacked Prince Derik, it was if he came out of nowhere." Lailii shook her head. "I don't know for certain if he has a Gate the other side of the mountain."

"Well, what I *do* know is that we can't travel any farther until her Moonfire has passed." He walked with Cruz to the edge of the pool. "I suggest you allow the men to hunt in small groups; it will keep their cats contented. Keep guards on the perimeter of our camp. Two nights is all I ask, and we can be on our way."

"I think for once you're wrong." Cruz sprang out of the water. "You're giving the Butcher ample time to arrange an ambush. I know just the place. If it were me, I would attack when we negotiate the pass, back through the mountains."

"Yes, in single file we would be vulnerable, but there may be a way to trick the Butcher into the open." Dallin shrugged. "I have no other choice but to wait. Moonfire lasts three days, and you know we must mate Lailii during this time. If we are attacked, our men are well equipped to deal with the Army of Lost Souls."

"You must trust in my powers for such an attack, my lord." Lailii lifted her chin.

Under his palms, Lailii straightened. Stryker brushed his lips across her pointed ear. Her scent filled his nose. How could such a small female think to take on an army? "You are so brave, sweetness."

"We will discuss your powers when the time comes, little one." Dallin smiled at Lailii.

"I'll go and see to the troops as you suggest." Cruz turned to leave. "And I'll have a meal sent to your tent. I can hear Lailii's stomach rumbling from here."

Lailii averted her gaze from the Pride's superb body. The scent of her males overpowered her senses. She looked up into Stryker's face. "I *really* can help."

"Don't worry about that now, sweetness." Stryker kissed a path down Lailii's ear. "Little darlin' . . . I have more pressing needs right now."

"So do I." Dallin sat on a large boulder. "Come here."

Without a second thought, she walked toward Dallin and stood before him. He drew her close and nibbled her lips. His hot mouth pressed against her chin, her neck, and then suckled each breast until her pussy wept. Lailii followed the path of a drop of water across the bite marks on his neck, down his massive chest to disappear inside his belly button. Her gaze rested on the mushroom helmet of his cock. She licked her lips with the desire to taste him, to run her tongue across the sticky slit. As if reading her thoughts, Dallin leaned back on his hands, exposing his long, delicious length. Lailii sucked in a breath and bent over to swipe her tongue across Dallin's shaft.

Behind her, Stryker groaned. His hands grasped her bottom, and his hot tongue lapped at her pussy. She writhed in pleasure under his expert touch. His warm breath brushed against her cool flesh, bringing sensual delight. With a groan, she ran her tongue from Dallin's apricot-shaped balls up the length of his massive cock and lapped across the top. His flavor burst in her mouth. She moaned in pleasure and took him deep. Dallin moved his hips, sliding his thick shaft between her lips. So hard, yet like silk over steel. Lailii grazed her fangs along the velvet length. Gods, he tasted so good. The thrill sent white-hot shivers to her pussy.

"Yes, like that, little one. Suck me deep; make me come." Dallin rolled his hips.

The head of Stryker's shaft pressed against her channel and entered in one glorious slide. He pressed his hot groin against her bottom, pushing his cock deep. The wonderful sensation shot straight to her womb.

"You are so tight, so fucking hot." Stryker thrust hard. "I can't wait to feel your mouth on *me*."

So much pleasure . . . . The now-familiar sensations fluttered in her belly, growing in intensity and curling around her clit. Lailii ran her fingernails across Dallin's balls and sucked harder. He groaned, sat up, and buried his long fingers in her hair. His scent poured over her. She shuddered with the desire to please him. Water bubbled around her legs in a gentle caress, the cool water a stark contrast to the fire surging through her. Stryker drove into her, his large hands hot against the flesh of her hips. The slap of bodies filled the air. Dallin growled deep in his chest. His cock pulsated in her mouth, and then covered her tongue with his delicious seed. The taste threw her over the edge; her pussy clenched around Stryker's thick shaft. Her legs trembled, and nothing mattered but the uncontrollable, erotic sensations swirling through her body.

"Yes, come for me, sweetness." Stryker thrust harder. "Your sweet pussy is begging for my load."

Lailii lifted her head and licked her lips. Pleasure cascaded through her pussy; her knees buckled. Stryker's warm hands slipped around her waist, and they fell back into the pool. Water covered her head. She pushed down with her feet and broke the surface. "That's not nice."

Dallin drew her into his strong arms and carried her from the water. She looked up into his handsome face. "Thank you."

"Let me dry you." Dallin placed her on her feet. "I'm sorry we allowed Cruz to bother you. It won't happen again."

"I don't believe he meant to harm me."

"Neither do I." Dallin reached for a towel.

"I don't think 'harm' was what he had in mind." Stryker strode from the pool and shook the water from his hair.

Lailii enjoyed the way Dallin dried every inch of her skin. Her stomach rumbled. "You also promised you would feed me when you returned from hunting."

"Your wish is my command." Dallin grinned and waved her toward the tent.

Chapter Seven

Two days later, Lailii awoke in the early hours of the morning to the soft noises of lovemaking. She understood these few days of concentrated sex were to placate her Moonfire. In truth, this morning, the ferocious lust had dulled into a satisfied glow. Her attentive lovers had worn her out. She knew they loved each other, and the fact made her a little jealous. Although she had been their priority, she caught the few passionate, stolen kisses between them, after they thought she was asleep.

During their first night together, Dallin had ridden Stryker, and the thought of watching them together again made her pussy hot. Since that time, they had kept their distance from each other, sleeping either side of her each night. She opened her eyes and gazed at them from under her lashes. The way they kissed, so hungry for each other, brought a soft moan from her lips. She bit down on her tongue. She need not have worried. The men were too involved in each other to hear her.

Dallin moved his large body around in the bed so that they lay head to toe. His full, luscious mouth closed over Stryker's cock. With a groan, Stryker lifted his tousled head and found Dallin's hard shaft. Lailii's gaze moved between the two bobbing heads and the stroke of large, masculine hands. She loved the sounds they made while giving and receiving pleasure. Her hand went to her soaking folds, one finger circling her throbbing clit. The sight before her so stimulated her, she cried out, exploding in climax with her men.

Stryker lifted his head. Gods, Lailii was awake. He and Dallin had decided to play down their need for each other until their mate had settled into a steady relationship with them. He sat up and smiled at her. "Good morning, sweetheart."

She stretched languidly like a satisfied cat, her lips curled in a smile. "I love seeing you together. When you kiss, it's so erotic."

"You don't mind?" Dallin rubbed a hand over his face. "We thought it could wait until we all get to know each other better."

"We should be home today, and then we can discuss it some more." Stryker met Dallin's sultry gaze and licked his lips. "What do you say, Dal?"

"Do you like to watch, little one?" Dallin rose up on one elbow and smiled at Lailii.

"I wish you would let me join in." Lailii ran her fingers around both her nipples. "When we get home, I want to try something special with you."

With a groan, Stryker crawled over to her. He sucked one of her rosy nipples deep into his mouth. A moment later, he lifted his head. "Tell me what you have in mind before I go insane with lust."

"I want to suck your delicious, hard cock, while Dallin fucks you." Lailii ran her nails down Stryker's back. "Is that possible?"

Stryker cleared his throat. Her words sent blood pounding into his shaft. "Oh . . . yeah, it's possible."

"Dallin." Cruz bellowed from outside the tent. "I need to speak with you."

Dallin slipped from the bed, walked naked to the tent opening, and pushed open the flap. "What?"

"The scouts have reported there is movement some miles from the mountain pass. We have to leave. If the Butcher's army is moving in that direction, we need to be through the pass and into the Gate before he arrives."

"I agree; tell the troops to break camp." Dallin rubbed the back of his neck and yawned. "Can you organize some food and coffee? It's been a long night."

"Sure." Cruz grinned like a monkey. "Was her Moonfire all that you expected?"

"Hell yeah, and then some." Dallin glanced behind him and lowered his voice. "She is kinda cute, don't you think?"

"Ah huh." Cruz winked. "They *both* are."

* * * * *

The early morning haze swirled around the horses' feet, drifting from the river in bands of white mist. Dallin moved Courage forward to lead the troops through the forest on a descent into the valley. In the distance, he could make out a spectacular, amber rock formation jutting out from dense undergrowth. The rock hung threateningly above a cramped, chalk walkway between the mountains. The steep side of the passage fell some fifty feet to a fast-flowing river. The only way through was in single file, leaving them vulnerable to any threat waiting on the other side.

Dallin indicated for Brad to scout ahead, and then pulled his troops to a halt. They blended into the edge of the forest. A crow with wings that shimmered blue-black in the sunlight fluttered down from a tree and strutted close to Dallin's horse. He grinned and turned to Lailii. "I bet he doesn't know we're all cats."

The Spellweaver's face was grim. Dallin touched her cheek. "Little one?"

"This is a dangerous place. Many have died in this valley." Lailii bit her bottom lip. "There are often bandits hiding among the rocks."

"It's the Army of Lost Souls I'm worried about. They have demon protection." Dallin gazed into the distance. "The Lady was insistent we protect you from Passio."

"Why do you think Passio wants me?" Lailii shot Dallin a worried glance. "If he thinks to make me a slave, I will fight him with my last ounce of magyck."

Dallin smiled at her. She had suffered so much hardship, then had to endure Moonfire with two insatiable mates, and yet she was still so damn gutsy. The female amazed him. "I can't imagine why a demon would want you, especially when the Lady offers you Her protection." He ran his hand down Courage's neck. "I would've thought no self-respecting demon would dare to tangle with a goddess."

"I agree." Lailii met his gaze. "Although, why did she send you and not perform a miracle to save me?"

Dallin shrugged. "Maybe it was the only way to get the three of us together. Let's face it, the odds of us finding you 3000 years in the past were more than remote, they were impossible." He squeezed Lailii's hand. "Don't worry about Passio; you're not alone now. My entire army is here to protect you."

"We're not like Prince Derik." Stryker scowled. "We'll die before the Butcher or any damn demon lays a hand on you."

The crow spread its wings and took to the air cursing. Dallin followed its flight, turning his head into the wind. A strong breeze brought a stench of unwashed male, accosting his Pride senses. He swore, turned Courage around, and silently signaled to his men to take cover. A horse, spewing streaks of white foam, broke cover, thundering toward them in a cloud of dust. Brad, face sheet white, guided his horse to Dallin's side. "Report."

"Mutant's—maybe a hundred of them." Brad swiped his forearm across his mouth. "Gods, they're eating human remains."

"What's your plan?" Cruz pushed his horse forward. "If we attempt the passage, we're toast."

Dallin turned his gaze on Lailii. "Do they have magyck?"

"No." Lailii lifted her chin. "Not magyck like us but they drink demon blood. It makes them hard to kill."

"Decapitation is the only way they stayed down." Stryker grimaced. "When we discovered that interesting point, killing them with a zap was easy enough."

"I doubt they will just stroll on through the passage and into our waiting arms." Cruz snorted. "We need to lure them out."

"I can do that." Lailii looked straight at Dallin. "I will protect you, my prince."

With a snarl, Dallin dragged Lailii off the back of her horse and across his thighs. He turned her to face him. "Let's get one thing perfectly straight. *I* am here to protect *you*. And knock off calling me 'my prince' and 'my lord'. I'm *Dallin* – for the Lady's sake, Lailii – I'm your mate."

Lailii drew a deep breath. Such dominant, male arrogance, what was she to do? *Stay calm and explain in terms he can understand.* "Dallin . . . it makes perfect sense for me to lure the Butcher into the open."

"No fucking way." Dallin snorted, and his eyes turned deep amber. "It's not worth the risk. We'll wait him out."

Cupping Dallin's face, Lailii met his angry gaze. "My magyck is strong, my *love*. You must trust my judgment in this matter." Under her palms, Dallin shook with anger. "Will you at least *listen* to my plan?"

"It won't make any difference." Stryker growled deep in his chest. "We're *not* putting you in danger."

With a sigh, Lailii glanced at Cruz. "*Please,* make them see reason. All I want is for them to listen to my plan."

"Let her speak, Dallin. What possible harm can it do?" Cruz rubbed his chin. "We don't have any other plans at the moment."

Without waiting for Dallin's permission, Lailii continued. "If you all remain hidden, I can ride—at a safe distance — toward the passage. The Butcher will have lookouts. As soon as they see me, they will report to the Butcher that I am alone. He will assume I am trying to return to Prince Derik. He won't be able to resist. As soon as the Army of Lost Souls is moving through the passageway — "

"No way." Dallin butted in, shaking his head.

Lailii glared at Dallin and pushed hard on his chest. "*When* they're in the passageway, I will call up the river to wash them into the valley. They will be dazed and easy to defeat."

"Do you *think* Argos can outrun a raging river?" Dallin snarled at Lailii. "I *don't* think so."

Not defeated, Lailii smiled sweetly. "Oh yes, Argos *will* get me to safety. How long do you think it would take a horse to reach the top of the valley, if you take into account that I will be in control of the river?"

"She could do it." Cruz grinned.

"At what cost?" Stryker shot Cruz a black look.

146

"Can you do this without any danger to yourself?" Dallin pulled Lailii close to his chest. "Tell me the truth, little one."

Holding up her hand, finger and thumb a hair's breadth apart, Lailii smiled. "Mayhap this much, but don't worry. I will call up the water, and then flee before it reaches the pass." She pointed to the rise opposite the river. "You should direct your men to the top of the hill flanking the valley."

"Stryker, she belongs to both of us; do you agree?" Dallin sighed. "I think it's a feasible plan."

"Very well." Stryker gazed down the valley. "But *you* should ride beside her. Can you cloak the horse as well as yourself?"

"Yes." Dallin turned to Cruz. "Move the troops to the top of that ridge."

The troops moved in silence toward the top of the chalky rise, sending up a wall of white dust, their armor glinting in the sunlight. Lailii watched them spread out along the top, a gold line prominent against the white hilltop. She turned to Dallin and shook her head. "You can't come with me. I can't protect you against the force of my magyck. *Trust* me, Dallin, and save your strength for the battle to come."

Dallin lifted Lailii onto her horse. He took the small, gold packet from his pocket and activated his armor. His head filled with visions of her swept away in a torrent of water. He swallowed hard and gave her a curt nod. "Go before I change my mind." He tugged at her hair. "When you return, little one, promise me you'll stay on the ridge. I'll require all my wits to fight. Stryker will have my back, and I need to know you're safe."

"As you wish." Lailii smiled sweetly. "Stay safe, life mates."

Lailii moved forward with unnerving confidence. As she entered the valley, sunbeams bathed her long, platinum hair, giving her an ethereal beauty. Gods, she looked so small and vulnerable atop her huge, white stallion. The boy's clothes did little to disguise her femininity. Dallin motioned for Stryker and Cruz to follow him and took his position with his men. He waited, heart thumping loudly. His fingers ached from gripping the reins. The only sounds in the valley were the clinks of horses' tackle, the chatter of birds, and the rush of water from the fast-flowing river. His gaze never left Lailii's progress. His courageous mate rode, head erect and eyes front, with one hand gripping Argos's mane.

"There at the mouth of the pass, can you see him?" Stryker leaned toward Dallin. "He's running back to the Butcher."

Dallin signaled to his men to draw their weapons. The air filled with the tension of impending battle; the troops' faces formed a sea of grim masks. In the valley, Lailii lifted her small arms. Immediately, a cold breeze blasted Dallin's face. Gods, he could hear her begin to chant as if she were sitting beside him.

"Can you hear that?" Stryker whispered.

With a nod to his friend, Dallin listened intently. The sky began to darken. Purple clouds appeared and turned into a swirling, black mass.

"Dear Lady, heed my words. Bring down your wrath on the unworthy." The wind whipped around Lailii, tangling her hair into writhing, silver snakes. She gazed into the heavens. "Give me the power to flush out the villains that would harm my Pride. Protect my mates, the ones chosen to lead the fight against evil. Rise up the river at my command, as so I say, so mote it be."

Lightning flashed, jagged, blue-white spears hitting the rocks beyond the pass in ear-splitting cracks. The Army of Lost Souls spilled into the passage, riding hard. A sound like a hurricane roared through the valley. Dallin glanced toward his men. The troops' horses nickered and shifted restlessly, but not one man moved out of position.

In the distance, between the mountains, a funnel of water rose up high in the air. Dallin held his breath. The screaming waterspout fell to the ground the second Lailii dropped her arms. Silver hair flying in the wind, the Spellweaver turned Argos toward the rise. Lailii flattened her small body against the horse's neck and galloped flat out across the valley floor and up the rise. Argos tossed his proud head and stumbled up the sharp incline, finally reaching the top. As Lailii disappeared behind a wall of troops in a cloud of white dust, Dallin let out his breath.

Screams from the Butcher's men and the thunder of panicked horses echoed from the passage. The Butcher of Anwyn, gnarled hand held high in the air, led his men into the open, his standard-bearer close on his heels. The roar of water soon muffled the screams from the Army of Lost Souls. Dallin watched in awe. A wall of water spewed from the crevice, hurling man and horse into the valley. Then with a mighty crash, a massive wave broke over the mountain, tossing the Butcher's legion like boats in a storm. The wave dissipated immediately, leaving man and horse staggering to find foot.

Dallin lifted his arm. "Charge!"

Stryker urged his horse forward. The magnificent stallion moved under him smoothly, taking the uneven ground in its stride. Dallin's troops split into two. Cruz took one half to cut off the retreating Army of Lost Souls before they reached the pass. The battle raged for hours; the valley ran red with blood. The air filled with the stench of blood and piss. The valley echoed the screams of the dying. The Butcher's men attacked with short swords but never alone, always two or three surrounded each man. The zaps were efficient, but Stryker's muscles cramped from punching with one hand and using his zap with the other. His body ached from the mutant's sword blows, but it would take a diamond-tipped sword to pierce the golden suit. Thank the Lady for the warhorse. The incredible beast knew which way to step to keep him seated. When all seemed lost, Glory would rear up and trample the enemy into the ground.

After dispatching another mutant, Stryker whirled his horse around to see the Butcher and four men surround Dallin. He kicked his horse forward to join the fight. A man wearing a black leather helm blocked his path. The stranger appeared, as if from thin air. Stryker looked into two empty eye sockets, and his heart pounded.

"You cannot win. Thy Lady will forfeit any battle to save your prince." The man laughed. "My master will come for your Spellweaver; there is no escape."

Stryker waved his zap at the man. "You got that wrong."

The man dissolved in a cloud of flies and vanished. Stryker shook his head and rode toward Dallin. The prince had decapitated four of the Butcher's men. The Butcher grinned weakly. The man's third eye was missing; black liquid spewed from a gaping hole in his chest. Dallin, face streaked with blood, raised his zap for the deathblow.

"The gate is open, and the lord of darkness has come to lead his children home." The Butcher lifted his chin. "My gift of the Spellweaver has been accepted by Lord Passio."

With a grimace, Dallin moved closer. "She belongs to us, given as life mate by the Lady. Damn you to hell." He lifted his zap and decapitated the Butcher in one pass.

The Butcher's head fell to the ground and rolled under the feet of the battling horses. His body slid to the dirt with a sickening thud. Dallin glanced around the battlefield. The remaining mutants in the Army of Lost Souls crumbled to dust. He put away his weapon and scanned the ridge. Lailii, standing like a welcome beacon in the sunlight, raised her hand in greeting. Dallin swallowed hard. "Gods, she is so beautiful."

"Don't forget talented . . . and she belongs to us." Stryker slapped Dallin on the back.

With a laugh, Dallin met Stryker's gaze. "I'm not going to forget *that* in a hurry. Gods, I'm falling in love with her."

"So am I." Stryker rubbed the back of his neck. "It's kinda scary, isn't it?"

"Yeah."

* * * * *

Lailii remained on the rise and gazed down on the sea of death. The mutants' bodies had turned to dust the moment Dallin dispatched the Butcher. However, the stench of battle remained. The troops moved to the river and stripped off their blood-soaked armor. Each one performed a spell to clean his soiled garments before diving into the water. There were few injuries, and not one of Dallin's men had died in the fight. She had watched, amazed at the magyck conjured by the Pride males. The zaps aside, she had witnessed the men produce spinning fireballs and others jumping from place to place to avoid

H.C. Brown – The Vane, Book One, Shifters and Demons

attack. Lailii knew such magyck existed, but in her time, only a Mage could perform such amazing feats.

An hour later, she followed the troops deep into the forest to rest and eat. Dallin dropped his saddlebags, spread a blanket on the forest floor, and fell onto it. Lailii frowned at him and offered him the wine skin. "You look exhausted."

"You think?" Dallin covered his eyes with his arm.

"We're all done in, sweetheart." Stryker sat down and handed Dallin a package of sandwiches. "We're not used to fighting mutants."

"I would have to say that was the worst battle I've ever experienced." Dallin sat up slowly and unwrapped his lunch. "There were so many of them; they just kept on coming." He broke off a portion of a meat sandwich and held it to Lailii's mouth. "It was the shadows that fazed me." Dallin pulled a face. "The twin suns make the shadows deceiving; half the time I thought someone was behind me, and it was my second shadow. It was creepy." He shrugged. "We

156

have two moons, so I'm used to the unusual shadows at night, but during a battle in daytime it's surreal."

Lailii opened her mouth for the food and chewed slowly. This custom of feeding her was ridiculous. Her men were exhausted. *It's pointless to argue.* She swallowed and glanced at Dallin. "I am surprised your magyck remained so powerful for the entire battle."

"We don't lose power." Dallin yawned and continued to feed her. "Our powers are from the Fae."

"I understand *you* are different to us." Striker held the wine skin to Lailii's lips. "Your powers are drawn from nature."

The cool, sweet Miza slid down Lailii's throat. She sighed. "Yes, from nature and from love. I am intrigued. How did cats get Fae powers?"

"The Fae and Prides are allies and have been for about two thousand years. It's not unusual for a Pride to find his life mate among the Fae." Striker passed the wine skin to Dallin. "My grandmother is Fae. Our bloods have mixed for many years and with that came the Fae magyck. The Vane was the first Pride to obtain the complete Fae talents. Now, all Pride — both male and female — have one special talent plus a variety of useful magyck."

Lailii smiled. To have an inexhaustible supply of magyck would be bliss. "I wish that were the case for me. I can sustain a spell for about an hour."

"I have a feeling that might change." Dallin offered Lailii another morsel of food. "The transformation is complete when you produce a cub. There have been Humans changed into Pride, and they have inherited magyck from their cat."

"You need not be concerned about your merging, sweetheart." Stryker touched Lailii's face and smiled. "At first, it seems unusual, but we all manage to live with our cats in perfect harmony."

Lailii swallowed and looked from one to the other. How could they possibly know what it was like without a cat inside their heads? "You don't know how I feel without a cat, so how can you possibly make that judgment?"

"We aren't born with our cats—well, we are, but they don't emerge until we mature." Dallin grinned. "Can you imagine a child changing into a cat? Hell, it would make the terrible two-year-old cub a force to be reckoned with, don't you think?"

"It is strange, at first." Stryker leaned his back against a tree and crossed his feet at the ankles. "The cat does what it is told. If you tell it to shut up, it remains silent. The only not so good part is the hunting." He met Lailii's gaze. "Then they take over completely; we just go along for the ride. They overrule any feeling of disgust we may have, of killing and devouring. It becomes as natural as eating a piece of fruit."

With a shrug, Lailii reached for the wine skin. At least they let her drink on her own. "It will be some time before I have a cub."

"Not necessarily." Dallin took her hand. "You could carry our cub already. A Pride female delivers in nine weeks."

Lailii opened her mouth to protest. One look at Dallin's intent gaze and she knew this was not a joke. "Nine weeks—that would mean I could have a cub *four* times a year. Dear Lady."

"No, our females only conceive once every two years." Dallin squeezed her hands. "You have nothing to fear, little one, I promise."

She snorted. "That's the exact reaction I would have expected from a man."

"Pride females suffer no pain in childbirth." Stryker stroked Lailii's hair. "We will help you care for our cub. In fact, you may find us too attentive."

"We will see." She met Dallin's gaze. "When do we leave for the future? Methinks I will find this a very strange adventure."

"The Gate is on the other side of the mountain, beside an ancient oak tree." Dallin sighed. "It will be very different for you. I am sure you will adjust nicely. The castle is very old, more like this time. If my father had his way, Vane Castle would remain authentic, but we do have modern technology. You will soon get used to our ways." He smiled. "I'll let my troops rest for an hour, and then we'll leave. As you mentioned, we may run into bandits. I need my men ready to fight."

An hour later, Dallin led the troops down into the valley and through the mountain pass. He glanced at Lailii; a spot of dirt marked her cheek. She would require a bath and clean clothes before he presented her to his father. He scratched his chin. The shops in the village below Vane Castle would have to do. There would be time later to buy her something better to wear.

They approached the old oak tree. In a whoosh of wind, a portal formed. Nothing like the usual expanse of shimmering silver of the travel Gates, the Lady's Gate swirled in a blue mist. Cruz gave him a broad smile and waved him through. Dallin knew his brother would wait until the last man had passed through in safety.

Dallin waited and watched his men file through the other side of the gate. They all whooped their relief to be on home soil again. He waved them toward the castle. Cruz appeared, grinning like a baboon, and the Gate closed behind him. Dallin led the way to the stable. He turned to Stryker. "We have to buy clothes for Lailii. We'll have to go into town before we take her to meet my father."

"Then we'll go now. How long can it take to buy a few dresses?"

Twenty minutes later, his patience at an end, Dallin turned Lailii to face him. "A flybike is like a horse. It is something you must accept. It's our main form of transport."

"People are *not* supposed to fly." Lailii balled her fists on her hips. "We should go by horse."

"The people will think we're crazy." Stryker snorted and looked away. "If you're going to be difficult over a flybike, you'll never fit into our world."

Dallin stroked her hair. His mate trembled under his touch. He met her clear, silver gaze. "You will love flying, little one. Trust me." He mounted his black, shiny flybike and patted the smooth leather seat behind him.

"Do I have any choice?" Lailii bit her bottom lip.

"Yes." Stryker swung his leg over a flybike. "Which one of us do you want to ride with?"

"You're a hard man." Lailii glowered at Stryker. "I choose to ride with Dallin."

"Ah huh." Stryker grinned. "I don't remember you complaining last night."

Lailii tossed her long hair over her shoulders and climbed gingerly behind Dallin. Her small arms closed around his waist like a vise; her nose dug into his back between his shoulders. He laughed. "You're safe with me. Just think about all the nice clothes I'm going to buy you. Girls love shopping, don't they?"

"Girls love to go shopping on horseback." Lailii complained. "Not flying about on this devil's magyck.

Gods, Dallin, how can it remain upright with only
two wheels?"

Dallin zapped the engine, and the flybike rose
silently into the air. He flew slowly to allow Lailii to
adjust to the sensation. She gripped him so tightly he
thought his brains might pop out the top of his head.
He turned to grin at Stryker. The man pointed to
Lailii and squeezed his eyes shut. Dallin ran a hand
down Lailii's thigh. "Don't be afraid. Look ahead not
straight down. It is like being on top of a mountain."

Lailii opened her eyes. Her stomach dropped.
They were descending into a town. Flybikes moved in
all directions like dragonflies above a pond. The
houses resembled boxes, each made from strange, red
stones, all the same exact size, and many had a front
with a great expanse of glass reflecting the sunlight.
The flybike drifted into a small area and fit snugly
into a line of similar contraptions. Stryker
dismounted, and then walked toward her and bent
his handsome face close to hers. She met his gaze, her

heart pounding. What else did they think to expose her to this day?

"You can let go now." Stryker laughed. "Poor Dallin is red in the face. I hope you haven't broken his ribs." He grabbed Lailii's waist and lifted her from the flybike.

Knees like jelly, Lailii gripped Stryker's arm. "I am a little shaken."

"You'll be fine." Dallin tipped his head to the right. "The shops are just across the road. When we get there, I'll ask someone to help you. In our time, it's easy to buy stuff when you know what size you are."

Lailii slipped her hands through her mate's arms, and they walked across the road. She caught her breath. Great, silver, egg-shaped things moved about the sky or slid to a halt along the roadside. The side would open with a hiss like an angry snake, and people would step out onto the road. She raised her head to look into the sky. Only one sun graced the heavens, and yet in the east, she could see the shapes of two ghostly moons.

The buildings were many and reached high into the clouds. They displayed a wide range of goods for sale, all protected behind a wall of windows. She followed Dallin through a glass door that opened at their approach, and then closed behind them. Inside, an abundance of fragrances filled the air. Clothes were displayed on statues of females. How strange. The people inside the shop drew back to let them pass and bowed low at the sight of their prince.

Dallin straightened his broad shoulders and spoke quietly to a pair of women. He turned and drew Lailii forward. His warm breath brushed her cheek. "Go with these females, and they will help you select some clothes. Remember your size. I will be taking you shopping again soon." He touched Lailii's hair. "They will take you to a special place, called a beauty parlor, and get you ready to be presented to the king.

"Spare no expense. I want her dressed as my princess. Make sure you have everything she needs delivered to the castle this afternoon, and I mean everything—hairbrushes, soap, shoes—whatever a female needs to be happy." Dallin's lips curled into a smile. "Call me when she is ready to leave; we'll wait in the Cat's Whiskers."

Lailii panicked. She grasped Dallin's arm. "You don't expect to leave me here alone, do you? What if Passio is close by?"

"That was a long time ago." Stryker laid a hand on Lailii's shoulder. "I think you will be safe here."

"We will do a little shopping, take a massage, and wait for you across the road in the tavern." Dallin pushed Lailii toward the waiting women. "Go and enjoy."

Go and enjoy? The men had lost their minds. She followed the females through rows of glass cabinets and areas filled with clothes hanging from silver bars. They went through more glass doors and finally into a small room with a female dressed in a white dress.

"This is Kate, my lady. She will get you out of those clothes and take you to the spa. When you are finished there, she will see to your hair and nails." One of the females gave her a broad smile. "We will collect a selection of clothes for you to choose from." She took a long ribbon marked with numbers from her pocket. "First, if you will allow me to take your measurements."

Three hours later, Lailii stroked down her pale blue silk gown and turned to gaze at her reflection in the long mirror. The dress, one of two dozen, reflected in her eyes. A split up both sides to the thigh showed an expanse of golden skin. Silver sandals, as soft as a dove's wing, encased her feet in tiny straps. Her nails shone with a coat of foul-smelling polish, and her hair hung down her back like a sheet of silk. A massive collection of clothes, shoes, and toiletries, piled high in boxes, sat by the door for delivery. She had delicate nightdresses of every hue and as thin as cobwebs. Her face grew hot at the thought of wearing such revealing attire, but the females had insisted her mates would love them.

"You are ready to leave, my lady." Kate moved to her side. "I am honored you chose our shop." She smiled. "Has the prince known you very long?"

Lailii laughed. *About three thousand years.* "Yes, I have known my mates for some time."

"You are truly blessed to have Sir Stryker as a mate, as well as our good Prince Dallin." Kate beamed at Lailii. "The Lady has certainly smiled on you."

Stryker led the way into the shop. He held out his arm to stop Dallin, and they both stared at Lailii. "Lady's blood, she looks like a goddess."

"An angel." Dallin moaned. "My only thought is to remove that dress and have her in our bed between us, damp and willing. Lady help me, I'm turning into a sex maniac. I thought the lust would settle with the end of her Moonfire."

With a shake of his head, Stryker turned to his lover. "I think my feelings are a little different. The last few days, I've felt as if I was addicted to her. Today, the deep cravings to mate have gone." He ran a hand through his hair. "Now, I feel love for her, right down deep in the pit of my stomach. I want to make love to her, long and slow. Do you know what I mean?"

"Uh huh. I sure do." Dallin rubbed his hands together. "We'll just have to push that need down until we've taken our vows. I want to have everything in order before we tell my father. As soon as we get back to the castle, I'll send for the Chancellor and Cruz. My father can't dispute our claim once witnessed."

Lailii looked at her mates standing in the doorway. They had taken one look at her, and then froze on the spot. Did she look so bad in a dress they had changed their minds about her? She took in their tight, black pants. Gods, the fine, charcoal material clung to their muscular thighs like a second skin and molded to their prominent sex. Dallin wore a dark blue shirt, and his hair hung like a sheet of black water down his back. Stryker had chosen a green,

H.C. Brown – The Vane, Book One, Shifters and Demons

sleeveless tunic to show off his strong, muscular arms. Brown curls tumbled over his shoulders, the gold highlights glistening under the overhead lights. Her stomach clenched. Their expressions were unreadable.

"Wow." Dallin grinned and walked forward. "You look sensational."

"You smell good too." Stryker moved to Lailii's side and ran a hand down her back.

She lifted her chin. "I'm surprised. Did you know they would cover me in mud?" She grimaced. "You have a very strange way of cleansing skin in this time."

The men grinned like baboons. Lailii glared at them. "Then they made me lie on a table and practically pummeled me to death." She folded her arms across her chest. "Stop laughing. This is no jest."

"We're not laughing at you." Dallin sobered. "We have other things on our minds."

"Ready to go, sweetheart?" Stryker offered Lailii his arm.

171

She looked from one delicious man to the other. If there was a crisis, they hid it well. Sliding her hands through their arms, she walked with them into the street. "I know there is something amiss; I can feel it."

"Not a problem, as such." Dallin took her hand. "It is our custom in the royal family to have our joining witnessed. I will make arrangements as soon as we get home."

"Then we will present you to the king." Stryker grinned. "There's nothing to worry about."

They walked along the street and into the parking lot. Lailii climbed onto the flybike behind Dallin. "I believe there is a problem. Do you think the king will be disappointed in your choice for a mate?"

"Nothing I do of late pleases him." Dallin zapped the flybike into life. "His Oracle predicted I would take a female from another Pride. I guess he just said that to make my father happy."

"The king is into the purity of the royal line." Stryker frowned. "Although, I can't say adding your blood would make any difference. They already have ancient Fae blood in their lines."

Lailii slipped her arms around Dallin's back. *Only Pride and Fae blood run through the royal veins. I'm guessing adding my lowly bloodline will make a great deal of difference to the king.*

Chapter Eight

Later that day, Lailii stood between her mates in a small chapel in Vane Castle. Her heart thundered against her ribs. The Chancellor, a stern, elderly man, dressed in black with a red vest, stood beside Cruz. A scribe sat at a nearby table with a massive leather-bound book open in front of him. On their return, Dallin had placed two identical gold talismans around his neck. These, he had explained, carried his royal seal. Only his chosen female could wear one of the royal amulets.

"Lailii of the Tark, will you promise to have Prince Dallin of Vane and Stryker of Talynx for all eternity?" The Chancellor's voice echoed in the small room. "Do you promise to have no other?"

Lailii swallowed hard. She lifted her chin to meet the old man's gaze. "I promise."

"Do you both give your promise to Lailii of the Tark?"

"I promise." Dallin placed one of the talismans over her head. "Let it be written that I also accept Stryker as my true mate, and all our cubs, no matter which male they favor, will be of royal blood."

"I give my promise to Lailii and Dallin." Stryker slipped his arm around Lailii's waist and squeezed. "For all eternity."

Dallin, and then Stryker, kissed her. Her head reeled with the passionate embraces. She heard Cruz laughing softly, and her face grew hot.

"I wish you happiness." The Chancellor smiled thinly and turned to the scribe. He dashed his signature across the Book of Royal Joining and then turned to Cruz. "Will you witness my signature, please, Prince Cruz?"

"Sure." Cruz grinned and added his mark to the page.

"Are you coming with us to see father?" Dallin caught Cruz's arm before he left the room.

"I wouldn't miss it." Cruz chuckled. "He is in the solar. Do you want me to pave the way for you?"

"Nah." Dallin ran a hand over his face. "Would you take Lailii out of harm's way, if things get nasty?"

"Not a problem." Cruz met Lailii's gaze. "If my father threatens to cut off your head, run to me."

Bile rushed up Lailii's throat. Cut off her head? Dear Lady, would it come to that? She nodded, too shaken to utter a reply. They followed the Chancellor from the room and along a wide passageway. The Castle reminded her of home. Black stone walls rose in peaked arches throughout the enormous building.

Magnificent rugs covered the floors, and the walls held paintings so real they could be windows into another world. Although old, even by her standards, the castle had every convenience. The modern marvels intrigued her. Water, so hard come by in her time, flowed from the walls through metal pipes. One pressed a button and water flushed a toilet, the contents vanishing to where she did not want to know.

The vid screens frightened her. When she asked what magyck locked the people inside the black glass, instead of explaining, her mates had rolled around laughing. Would seem her difficulty in understanding fueled their hilarity. Now she must meet a king who may order her decapitation. Perhaps life in the future was not so rosy, after all.

By the time they climbed the stairs and walked along the red carpet to the king's solar, Lailii wanted to run away and hide. Her knees trembled, and her stomach threatened to empty right there on the king's splendid rug. Dallin introduced her, and she curtsied low, not rising until the king gave permission. The king, a grey-haired version of Dallin, reclined in a large, leather chair. Unlike Dallin, the king's face bore lines of sadness. His mouth turned down at the corners, and his face appeared cast in stone.

"You introduce this maid as Lailii of the Vane. Do my ears deceive me, or have you taken this child as your life mate?" The king got to his feet. "The Lady's rules are quite clear. No female under the age of eighteen summers is to be considered."

"Lailii is nineteen summers, Father, and yes she is given to Stryker and me as life mate." Dallin reached for Lailii's hand. "We have registered our joining. We come here for your blessing."

"Blessing." The king bellowed. "Look at her. She is a naught but a wood nymph. Do you honestly believe she will produce suitable princes for the Vane or a warrior heir for the throne—a leader of all the Prides?" He snorted. "You've let your cock rule your head. Mark my words, this is a mistake. The Oracle has spoken. You are destined to take a warrior bride with clean bloodlines."

Lailii trembled. The king's booming voice hurt her ears. She glanced at Dallin. Her mate's face was sheet white. His large hand squeezed her fingers. Stryker's warm palm cupped her elbow, and she leaned into him for support. The king would put her to death to break their bond. She bit her bottom lip until blood leaked into her mouth.

"How dare you insult Lailii?" Dallin straightened his shoulders. "She is a Spellweaver, not a damn wood nymph. Her bloodlines will enhance our own with ancient magyck. You knew the Lady sent me to retrieve her from 3,000 years in our past, and now we know the reason why. In truth, we were delighted to discover Lailii was our mate." He smiled at Lailii. "She belongs to Stryker and me, and we love her. Nothing you can do will ever change that, Father."

"What a load of crap." The king banged his fist on the table. "Do you really think I would believe such an outrageous lie? It's inconceivable to believe the Lady would dishonor the Vane in this way. This . . . this . . . *Elf* is not a suitable match for my heir. And . . . I find it hard to believe something this . . . *inconsequential* has any talent for magyck—let alone powers to enhance what the Vane took thousands of years to achieve."

"It is true, sir." Stryker straightened his back. "We fought and killed the Butcher of Anwyn and, without Lailii's magyck, we would have lost many lives. Our troops will tell you the same story."

"I was there." Cruz stepped forward. "Everything Dallin says is true. Lailii has amazing powers. Ancient powers. We are lucky to have her in the family."

"Did I ask for your opinion?" The king glared at Cruz, then turned his attention back to Dallin. "Where did you find the girl?"

"The Lady sent us to rescue her from a dungeon." Dallin frowned. "She was near death."

"How long was she held prisoner?" The king rubbed his chin.

"Six months." Dallin sighed. "My bite made her whole."

"That is a long time for a female to be alone with mutants. What proof do you have that she does not carry a foul cub?" The king met Lailii's gaze and nodded slowly. "Yes, a pretty little thing like you would be a temptation no guard could resist. Chained up and deep in a dungeon where no one could hear your screams, you would be fair game."

"No." Dallin growled deep in his chest. "She was untouched."

"We shall see." The king turned his back and pressed his hands on the table. "If she produces a mutant, both she and the cub will burn." He turned and glared at Lailii. "Know this, Spellweaver, the Vane carry a royal birthmark placed by the Lady, so don't think you can fool me with a bastard."

"Have you finished?" Dallin snarled. "This is the future queen of the Vane you're insulting."

"For now." The king lifted his chin and glared at his son. "Make the most of the next few days with your mate. I've received reports of mutants causing trouble in Landsdown. The raids are becoming more frequent. I have reason to believe a demon has opened a portal with the intent to feed on my people. I sent Broderick and a few men to scout it out yesterday. As soon as he returns, you will be leading a battalion to drive them back to the Underworld."

Lailii shot a glance at Dallin. She would go with him. A Spellweaver must protect their prince. She gave him a small smile. He returned her gesture with a shake of his head. Her heart sank. He planned to leave her here with his mad man of a father. She drew a deep breath to complain, and then bit back the words.

"As you wish. Send Broderick to me with the details on his return." Dallin shrugged. "I think I'm becoming an expert on killing mutants." He ran a hand through his hair. "Is that all, Father?"

"Yes." The king waved them away. "Get out of here."

Stryker waited until they had walked down the stairs, and then turned to Dallin. "That went well."

"He's afraid." Dallin led the way into the great hall. "He's an old man. When he met my mother, he was over two hundred summers. He only wants to ensure our bloodline."

"Funny way of showing it."

"It's the way he is, and he'll never change." Dallin drew Lailii close to his side. "Don't worry, little one. My father rarely leaves his solar, so we won't have to tolerate his biased opinions every day."

"What about your mother?" Lailii frowned. "Will she shun me as well?"

"Mother is . . . unpredictable." Dallin sighed. "We'll keep you away from her for as long as possible."

Stryker shot a glare at Dallin. "Tell her the truth." He turned to Lailii. "Don't expect her to like you. She hates me because I'm a Talynx. Thank the Lady the castle is big enough to avoid Dallin's parents."

"I am unwelcome, and yet you expect me to remain here while you go to Landsdown?" Lailii met Dallin's gaze.

"Yes. It won't be so bad." Dallin rubbed her back. "I'll only be gone a week, at the most."

"I want to ride beside you. I am a Spellweaver. It is my place to be beside my mates." Lailii frowned. "Have you lost interest in me so soon?"

Taking her hand, Stryker looked into her troubled eyes. "Sweetheart—that will *never* happen."

"We love you, and that won't change as long as we live. Trouble is, little one, you've been through enough these past months, and we don't want you in danger." Dallin sighed. "We can't be sure if Passio is behind the mutant raids. The Lady did mention he could travel through time. It could be a trap. It's safe here, even if you have to put up with my parents."

"I won't know what do here alone. I don't know anybody." Lailii gripped Dallin's arm.

"I will arrange a tour of the castle for you." Dallin smiled. "I want you to be happy. The entire north wing belongs to me. Will you make it into a home for us? Can you do that for me?"

"I would love to do that, but please, Dallin, I don't want to stay here without you. I don't know your ways," Lailii replied.

Stryker shot Dallin a glare. Their mate was on the point of becoming hysterical.

"You won't have to interact with anyone you don't know until we return." Dallin covered Lailii's hand. "You can stay in the north wing the entire time, so there is nothing to worry about, little one."

Inside the great hall, the room hummed with conversation. Dinner at the castle was always a friendly affair. Stryker paused at the royal table. The aroma of freshly baked bread, roasted meat, and pumpkin soup wafted under his nose. His stomach rumbled. He pulled out a chair for Lailii. The female's face was chalk white. He smiled at her. "We aren't going tomorrow. I'm guessing it will be over a week before we leave. We'll have time to show you around and make sure you're settled."

"Relax." Dallin smiled and sat down beside Lailii. "And smile. My people will think we're arguing."

Stryker laughed. Lailii's grin was like a grimace. He moved closer and whispered in her ear. "I want you to imagine a real bed with me and Dal making passionate love to you all night."

He watched her cheeks color. "I can't wait to taste you again. I want to run my tongue up your inner thigh right now." He touched her leg. "Will you suck me while Dallin takes my ass?"

"Stryker . . . please." Lailii glared at him.

With a chuckle, Stryker reached for the soup. "Hey, Dal, don't you love it when she begs?"

"Oh, yeah." Dallin groaned.

* * * * *

After dinner, Stryker took Lailii's hand and led her from the great hall. "I'll show you our rooms. Dallin is organizing a maid for you."

"I don't want a maid." Lailii lifted her chin. "I am perfectly capable of dressing myself, thank you." She turned to look at Stryker. "I don't believe I will enjoy having another female close to my mates."

Jealousy. That has to be a good sign. Stryker led her up a winding staircase and through a heavy wooden door into the north wing. "When we're away, you will need a female to escort you around the castle and to arrange meals and the like. We can hardly leave a male, can we?" He stopped to speak to the guards. "Prince Dallin has taken Princess Lailii as his life mate. He is on his way with your orders."

The guards bowed respectfully and allowed them to pass into the hallway. Lailii glanced around. Apart from the odd landscape painting and walls of ancient weaponry, this part of the castle held nothing of comfort. No wonder Dallin expected her to make this barren wing a home. She wondered how he could have lived here so long without at least some modicum of furnishings.

She followed Stryker. A blast of cold air sent a shiver down her spine. "Where is that breeze coming from?"

"That would be the arrow slits. Most of them are covered, but Dallin hasn't lived here for the past few years, so I guess the king didn't bother to do any maintenance. The rooms will be clean and the bed linen fresh. Dallin gave orders before he left."

The corridor turned a sharp left, and Stryker stopped outside a very plain wooden door and smiled brilliantly at her. "This is our room." He pushed open the door and stood to one side to let Lailii pass. "It's made for comfort."

Lailii stopped in the doorway and peered inside. Thick, burgundy rugs covered the floor. She stepped into a comfortable sitting room, with long, beige leather sofas arranged around a low table.

Through an open door, Lailii could make out a massive bed. "This looks very nice. What other rooms are available?"

"Open any door." Dallin appeared behind them. "The entire north wing is ours." He opened his arms wide.

With a gasp, Lailii clamped her hand over her mouth. This new magyck would take a little getting used to. She drew a deep breath and turned to Dallin. "You startled me. I assume you jumped here?"

"Yes. I do so frequently inside the castle; it's quicker than walking." Dallin took Lailii's hand.

"How exactly *do* you jump?"

"It's not a difficult spell but one that must be used with caution. You can't jump to a place you're unfamiliar with, or you may end up inside a wall—or worse, inside a solid object—then you're toast." Dallin turned her around to face him. "We usually start by jumping from one spot in a room to another. You must picture the place you want to land in your head and picture it empty. Jumping on top of someone is considered extremely rude."

Lailii grinned. She would love to learn this remarkable spell. First, she wanted to explore her new home. "When can I see the rest of the castle?"

"You will have plenty of time to explore tomorrow. Come and see our rooms." He led her across the sitting room. "The bedroom is through there, and we have a bathroom with a sunken hot tub."

Sunken hot tub? "It all looks very nice." Lailii glanced at the huge, black screen. "I will try and get used to the vid screen. Unfortunately, I have a hard time believing the people aren't watching us from inside some strange hell."

"I promise you they're not." Stryker laughed. "We do have communication devices that have live images. I will explain those later."

A strangled growl emanated from across the room. A flash of black fur bounced toward Dallin. Lailii threw a ball of white magyck at the beast, and it hit the floor with a loud thud, talons digging long trails in the polished wood floor. The catlike creature spun on its feet, then hunched in a crouch. Four green eyes flashed in annoyance; the long rat-tail flashed from side to side. Tall ears flattened against a rounded, black velvet skull. Long whiskers stuck out like barbs. The beast let out a blood-curdling yowl and bared long, white fangs. Lailii held up her hand to ward off the attack. "Gods, what is that?"

"That would be Buzz." Dallin moved toward the snarling beast and lifted it into his arms. "She is a Loop and my pet since childhood." He rubbed the Loop's ears. "She won't hurt you."

"Don't listen to him." Stryker dragged Lailii away from Dallin. "That thing is a demon."

The Loop rubbed its head against Dallin's cheek, purring in welcome. It climbed onto his shoulder and shut one pair of eyes. Lailii relaxed. This was a protective pet, nothing more. She would try to make friends with the creature. She moved closer to

Dallin and held her hand out to the Loop. "Hello, Buzz."

To her amazement, Buzz nuzzled her fingers. Dallin gave her a cheeky grin, lifted the Loop from his shoulder, and placed it on the floor. Lailii smiled at him. "I'm guessing she doesn't like Stryker?"

"She keeps out of his way." Dallin laughed.

"I have the scars to prove otherwise." Stryker pointed to a white scar on his arm. "I'm glad she likes you, sweetheart." He glared at Dallin. "Can we get on with the tour? I want to get our mate to bed; she's exhausted."

"There are connecting rooms to my bedchamber." Dallin moved into the bedroom and indicated a far door. "I suggest you use one as a dressing room. In fact, I have already arranged for your maid—an older female called Jessie—to tend you. She will have all your new clothes unpacked this evening." He smiled down at her. "I have two squires; I will leave one here. You must ask him for whatever you need to make the rooms to your liking."

Lailii bit her bottom lip. This was a male domain. Dark wooden furniture, polished to a high shine, glistened in a stream of moonlight pouring through a window with heavy, velvet drapes. The bed would sleep six. Her pussy quivered at the thought of making love to her mates within the luxurious blankets. She lifted her chin. "Where, pray tell, do I find a carpenter to make furniture?"

"You can access the shops' entire catalogue on the vid screen." Dallin ran a hand over Lailii's back. "My squire will show you. Just tell him what you require, and he will arrange delivery to the castle. I'll have men at your disposal."

He expected her to buy items in his name. Lady forbid. What would happen if she purchased something he did not like? Gods, she could not do this alone, not in this new world with all its strange rules and flying machines. She met Dallin's gaze. "No, I think not. I have no idea of the items required. This time is very different from my own. I will wait and seek your guidance. We will all make a home here, together."

"Sure." Dallin touched her cheek. "Whatever makes you happy, little one."

Lailii moved across the room and opened the connecting door. The adjoining room was a bedchamber with another massive bed, complete with red silk sheets and lace-trimmed pillows. She raised a brow and turned to her mates. "Do you expect me to sleep in here? It looks like a harlot's bedchamber."

"Yeah, well." Dallin swallowed hard. "I preferred to have my liaisons in this room."

"You paid for sex with harlots?"

"Yes. It was difficult as Prince Royal to find a suitable bed partner, especially a female who would be willing to take on both of us at the same time." Dallin growled. "I'm a male, damn it; I need sex often. This special room close to my bedchamber was the best choice."

Trying hard not to grin, Lailii set her gaze on his bouncing Adam's apple. She cared less that he had females in his past. He belonged to her now, they both did, and that was all that mattered. She would enjoy Dallin's explanation. "Oh, and why is that?"

"So I could walk away and shut the door." Dallin rubbed the back of his neck. "It was just sex."

Lailii watched spots of color stain Dallin's cheeks. Stryker had suddenly found a painting of a battle scene extremely interesting. "I asked if you expected me to sleep in here; you haven't answered my question. Do I assume from your answer that you want to hide from me, also?"

"Gods no." Dallin took two steps toward her, wrapped her in his arms, and crushed her to his chest. "We want you in our bed every night." He waved a hand toward the bed. "I'll have that damn thing removed first thing in the morning."

With a grin, Lailii buried her face in his chest. She inhaled his scent and sighed. "Thank you."

Dallin lifted her into his arms. He had waited long enough; he desired her. Now. He walked into his bedchamber, placed Lailii on the bed, and then pulled off her shoes. He smiled at Stryker. "Lock the doors."

He tore off his clothes, and then rolled onto the bed, gathering Lailii in his arms. He inhaled her scent and slanted his mouth over hers. She responded, meeting every stroke of his tongue. Such a passionate female. With one kiss, she was ready for him. He could smell her feminine heat. The bed dipped. Stryker gave a long sigh and lay down beside Lailii. Dallin cupped his lover's head, drawing him closer to Lailii—she belonged to both of them. Dallin kissed a path down her neck and lapped at the pounding vein in her throat. Under him, Lailii arched her back. Stryker gave Dallin a feral grin and expertly peeled Lailii's straps off her shoulders. The gown fell to her waist, exposing, full, pale globes. Stryker groaned and began to suckle her taut nipple. Dallin slid down in the bed to take the other tight bud in his mouth. Lady's blood, Lailii's breasts grew bigger by the day, and her nipples had colored to dark cherry. She tasted so damn sweet he could not get enough of her.

Stryker's long fingers curled in his hair. Dallin lifted his head to accept the man's mouth. Their tongues tangled in a rough, demanding kiss. Dallin dragged his mouth away, breathing heavily. "I so want your ass."

"I've thought of nothing else all day." Stryker licked his lips. "I'll sixty-nine Lailii so she can watch." He touched Lailii's cheek. "You want to suck me, sweetheart, while Dallin fucks my ass?"

"I'd like that." Lailii pulled off her gown and tossed it onto the floor. "Show me what to do."

"Turn around, lie on your back." Stryker crawled over Lailii and buried his face in her pussy.

Dallin reached into the nightstand drawer for the lube. He turned back toward the bed. Gods, he could come just watching them pleasure each other. To think Lailii knew nothing about sex just a few days ago. He climbed onto the bed and bent to press kisses across Striker's ass. He grazed his fangs across the man's suntanned flesh and met Lailii's gaze. "You look so sweet sucking on his cock."

With a growl, he knelt behind Stryker and covered the man's tight star with lube. Dallin fisted his shaft and eased it slowly into his lover's hole. So deliciously hot, Stryker's ass closed around him in welcome. Taking Stryker's hips, he drove into him. The man purred and pushed back, meeting every deep plunge. Lailii's small hands closed around his thighs, her fingers a gentle caress. Intense heat surged up his legs; gods, he had lost all control. He rode Stryker like a maniac. The room moved in and out of focus, his legs trembled, and he came. He wiped the sweat from his brow. "Shit." He slipped from Stryker and fell onto the bed next to his lovers. "Sorry."

"Don't be." Stryker grinned. "You were fantastic. I like it when you're out of control."

Stryker crawled off Lailii and turned her around. "That was brilliant, sweetheart, but let me love you now."

Lailii looked at him with an expression of bemused pleasure and licked her red, swollen lips.

Stryker moved between her legs and sank into her wet, hot pussy in one glorious slide. He bent to take her mouth, delighting in the mingled taste of both of them. Her sharp fingernails dug into his shoulders with his every deep, satisfying dive. Her hard nipples pressed against his chest. He took her long and slow until she shattered beneath him, crying out his name. Then he let the pleasure engulf him, and he rode out his climax in her pulsating channel. He wanted to stay inside her, and supporting his weight on his elbows, he licked circles around her red nubs. "You taste so sweet; I could lie here forever."

"Why don't you carry her into the hot tub?" Dallin stood by the side of the bed. "We'll have some wine and start over."

"You both need to be gentle with my nipples." Lailii cupped her breasts.

"Are they sore?" Dallin frowned.

"Yes, and my breasts feel very heavy."

Stryker rose to his knees. He ran a hand through his hair and shot a glance at Dallin. "How long has it been since the beginning of her Moonfire?"

"Six days, I guess." Dallin rubbed his chin. "You thinking what I'm thinking?"

"What are you thinking?" Lailii looked from one to the other.

With a grin, Stryker gathered Lailii into his arms. "We think you're carrying our cub. You have all the signs."

"No—it's too soon to tell." Lailii placed a hand on her belly.

"It's not if you're Pride. In eight weeks, you will be a mommy." Dallin bent to kiss her and then Stryker. "This is wonderful news."

"And you still plan to leave me here alone?" Lailii sighed.

Stryker lifted her into his arms and headed for the hot tub. "Of course, now more than ever you need to stay close to home. We can't risk you or our unborn cub."

* * * * *

Dallin stood in the courtyard beside his flybike, Stryker at his side. The week they had spent with Lailii had flown by too quickly. She stood at the entrance to the keep, her face a mask of sadness. One small hand pressed against the small bump in her belly. The cub had already made his presence known with strong kicks. Dallin knew deep in his heart the cub was male—their son, and the heir to the Vane Empire.

He deliberately held the news of the cub from his father. This announcement could wait until they returned. He pushed down the desire to go to her again and offer comfort. His gut clenched, and anxiety fogged his brain. He noticed Stryker's glum expression and knew he felt the same. Lailii was as important as the air he breathed. Gods, he wished he could stay. He met her gaze. She bit her full, bottom lip and raised her chin. With a nod, he climbed onto his flybike and led the battalion into the air.

* * * * *

Two weeks dragged by and Lailii grew afraid. How much longer would they stay away? If she had accepted the communication device Dallin had offered, she would know what was happening. What a fool she was to refuse a means of contact with her mates. She must try to overcome her fear of technology. Swallowing hard, she thought of the holographic image of Stryker smiling from the small, silver device. To see her mate's head floating without a body still brought night terrors.

After another week without news, she asked Dallin's squire, Peter, to obtain an Ocular phone. Red-faced and flustered, he informed her that the king had given orders to prevent her placing requests. The king would supply food and nothing else. Lailii hugged her stomach, suddenly afraid for her unborn cub. Out of her mind with worry, Lailii began to ask the servants each morning for news of her mates.

Tears came easily, and she could not eat. The young squire, on her maid's insistence, informed her that the king received calls almost daily from Dallin. She swiped at the tears running down her cheeks. "Have they sent a message for me?"

"Not that I know of, my lady." Peter met her gaze. "They are closing the demon gates—that is all I discovered."

Her heart broke into a million pieces. Surely, they knew she wanted to know they were safe. At least she assumed they were both well. Gods, she missed them. She craved their scent, the touch of their skin against her at night. Flinging herself on the bed, she pulled their tunics to her nose, inhaled, and let out a sob. A soft purr close to her ear made her lift her head. Buzz's damp nose nuzzled her cheek. The Loop knew her master was safe.

I need to see them, even if it is in a hologram. She slid off the bed and walked into the adjoining room.

Opening the door to the sitting room, she informed the guard she wanted to speak to Dallin's squire. The young man arrived five minutes later with a tray of afternoon tea. He set it down on the table and turned his flushed face toward her. Lailii smiled. Peter had tried valiantly to keep her company. "What information do you have for me today?"

"I know they are well. They found a fissure deep in the earth at the foot of the Banin Mountain. They believe the mutants gain access to our realms through that portal." He met her gaze. "The guards spotted me at that point and threatened to tell the king I was spying on him."

Lailii laid her hand on her belly. "I thought they would be home by now. I need to use the king's Ocular phone"

"The king will likely behead me if I make that request." The color drained from Peter's face.

She lifted her chin. "Then I will ask the king myself."

"I don't think that is wise." Peter frowned.

"Is he in his solar?"

"I believe so."

Rising from the chair, Lailii pursed her lips. What could the king do? She only wanted to know if her mates were well. "Give me a second to wash my face, and then take me to him."

* * * * *

Lailii waited outside the king's solar, her gaze moving to the dour faces of the guards. The door opened, and Peter ushered her inside. The king stood before the fireplace. His hard mouth formed a thin line. His broad shoulders were straight, his hands clasped behind his back. Lailii curtsied.

"I see your belly swells with a foul cub." The king glared at Lailii's stomach. "My son may be bewitched by you, but I see through your ploy. You infiltrated my kingdom to plant a demon seed into my line. Didn't you think I would recognize the link between you and the mutant invasion?" He drew a deep breath. "I have ruled this realm for over two hundred years, and until you showed up with your pretty little face, the demons left us alone."

Shocked by his outburst, Lailii took a step backward. The man's eyes filled with hate. Instinctively, she gathered her magyck around her, fear making her fingers crackle with white power. "I have not bewitched Dallin. Nor could I do any such thing. I am not a witch, sire." She placed a hand protectively over her belly. "This cub is your grandchild. I was a virgin when Dallin bit me."

"Ha! Magyck can do many things and fool many people, and you *are* a Spellweaver." The king scowled. "I believe you are a demon in the guise of a foundling." He glared at her hands. "Your magyck can't protect you in Vane Castel. I am the law here, and I will deal with your fate when Dallin returns. This estrangement will have broken your hold on him. I will make sure this never happens again. Get back to your room before I have you burned at the stake."

Lailii pressed her hand to her mouth and fled back to her room. Not fifteen minutes later, two guards arrived with a smithy. The old blacksmith held two bands of silver and an expression of distaste. Using all her power, Lailii cast a spell to protect her cub. A warm glow infused her belly, creating an impenetrable barrier against harm. She stood motionless and allowed the smithy to band her wrists with silver. The white metal burned into her skin, cutting off her magyck. With a cry of distress, she stumbled into a chair. Such cruelty . . . the king was no better than the Butcher was.

"Gather her things together; the king has ordered her to the dungeon." One of the guards barked at Peter. "We'll be back to collect her in half an hour."

"My lady." Peter knelt beside the chair. "Prince Zane and Kaden arrived home this morning. They know of the love Prince Dallin has for you; I was privy to the phone conversation. I will speak to them on your behalf. They will contact Prince Dallin and inform him of this disaster."

Lailii touched his young face. "Thank you. At least you believe me."

"I believe you too." Jessie bustled around collecting clothes. "The king knows nothing about you to make such a decision. Dear Lady, silvering went out in the Dark Ages; what is the man thinking?"

Lailii stared into space. *Dallin, Stryker where are you?*

* * * * *

Banin Mountain.

Dallin cloaked and moved closer to the fissure. The evil-smelling gas pouring from the deep crevice told him mutants used this Gate. He peered into the swirling mist and met a pair of red, glowing eyes. Heart thumping, he pulled away and jumped back to his camp. The adrenalin rush did little to stop the bone-deep weariness from two weeks of battle. He needed to go home; the separation pain from being away from his mate had become intolerable, his concentration fuzzy. Straightening his shoulders, he uncloaked and walked toward Stryker and Cruz. "Demon, I have no doubt. I can feel dark magyck surging around the fissure." He rubbed the back of his neck. "It's bigger than the last Gate. I'm not sure we can melt enough rock to seal it."

"We could cover it with some mesh. It would be easy enough to fix it into the rock. Nothing will get through a silver barrier." Cruz met Dallin's gaze. "Call Father and tell him what we need."

With a shrug, Dallin pulled out his Ocular phone. The king answered immediately. Dallin cleared his throat. "We have a problem. We need a barrier made of silver. I'll send a couple of men back with the specifications. How is Lailii?"

"She is well and sends her love." The king's hologram smiled. "Do you have a message for her?"

"Yes, the same message as always, that we love her. Tell her we will be home soon."

Dallin shut the phone and pushed it into his pocket. "I'll have to go back and measure the damn Gate." He grabbed at a nearby tree branch and snapped it off. "Help me strip the leaves off. I'll lay it across the fissure to measure the width. The height is easily as tall as I am, so say six foot five."

"You put yourself in danger every time you go there alone." Stryker stripped leaves from the branch. "At least let me watch from the rocks."

"You can't watch me when I'm invisible." Dallin grinned. "Don't worry; as soon as we seal this Gate, we're leaving. I need to bed my mate."

"Our mate." Stryker gave Dallin a crooked smile.

With the stick in one hand, Dallin cloaked and returned to the fissure. The air around him grew cold, and icy tendrils of fog swirled around his feet. Heart bouncing against his ribs, he moved closer and extended the branch across the gaping maw. A force hit him hard in the chest. He dropped the stick. Another blast lifted him high into the air and flung him toward the ground. He lay on his back, stunned by the impact. Freezing mist closed in around him. He fought for air. Invisibility deserted him, and the world folded to blackness.

Chapter Nine

Underworld

Passio grinned. At last, a pawn to use in negotiations with the king of the Vane. He gazed down at the body of Crown Prince Dallin. The king would trade a lowly Spellweaver for his son and heir. The damn king had stuck his nose into his business long enough. How dare he tamper with his Gates? What harm did he do to the man? In truth, he did the realms a service by taking those who chose to serve him. His mutants only fed on the weak, so no harm done. Surely the Pride king understood the law of the jungle — the survival of the fittest?

He ran a finger across Dallin's lips. On the other hand, this fine specimen would make a delicious addition to his bed. Passio laughed. "I can't lose."

What a wonderful position to be in. Passio motioned to his guards to revive Dallin. He stood in front of the naked man, and his sex grew hard. The prince enjoyed males. He had watched him with Stryker. Soon, the sweet prince would be begging for his cock.

"What the fuck." Dallin opened his eyes and struggled against the guards. "Where am I?"

Passio ran his flogger down Dallin's chest, across his flat stomach, and down to his impressive dick. He licked his lips. "You are in the Underworld. Don't try to use magyck because such an action brings extreme pain." He tapped the leather flogger on

Dallin's flaccid shaft. "You are an attractive man. I would like you on all fours, begging me to fuck you."

Dallin shook his head. If this was a demon, it was not what he expected. The sickly sweet scent of violets surrounded a young man with gentle features. Fair hair tumbled down his back. Not large and intimidating but small and effeminate, he dressed in blue silk and lace. The eyes changed from black to red. Dallin lifted his aching head and met the demon's gaze. "It's not gonna happen. Who the fuck, are you? Why have you kidnapped me?"

"I could *make* it happen. Many chose my bed over my rack. My name is Lord Passio." The demon inclined his head. "You are here to trade for Lailii of the Tark."

Lady's blood. Dallin drew himself up to his full height. "Lailii belongs to me, given to me as life mate by the Lady. She didn't send me into the past to rescue Lailii just to let you bring her to this hellhole.

Am I assuming you plan to go head-to-head with the Lady over my mate?"

"The Lady abandoned her daughter to the mortal world. It was Her choice to make her earthbound. The Spellweaver carries white magyck from the goddess. I need her magyck to walk on the earth. I'm sick of the constriction of this place. How can I feed with any dignity with the ten minutes I'm allowed above ground?"

What on earth was this idiot talking about? Dallin shrugged, and the movement made is captors crush him in a death grip. "She is a simple Spellweaver, nothing more."

"She is immortal, you fool." Passio ran the flogger through his fingers. "She will provide an eternity of power for me. I have everything she needs to regenerate her powers. Music, art and in the future, my love . . . she will love me; they all love me eventually."

Dallin chuckled. "You are the fool. If she were an immortal, she wouldn't have needed my help to escape the Butcher. She would have used her goddess magyck. It's laughable to think you really believe she would give up her powers to a demon. And, in case you don't understand about Pride mates. Lailii is incapable of loving any other now that she is mated to Stryker and me."

"My bite will fade the connection to you. My lover, Kaos, will feed from her as well. Soon, she'll crave only our touch." Passio shook his head slowly. "Your faith in the Lady is commendable. I loved Her once. Where do you think demons come from, Dallin? We are all gods who fell out of favor with the Great One. He created the Underworld to hold his brother, Baltor. The fool thought he could rule the realms. His crime and we all suffer the same punishment. We feed on mutants but crave the sweet blood of the innocent."

Dallin snorted. "I wasn't born yesterday. I know demons created the Vampire myth to cover their feeding frenzy in our worlds."

His stomach churned; the demon's smell confused his senses. He trusted in the Lady, he knew the love his mate held for him. There was no way Lailii would fall for this person. Demons were liars; everyone knew that—right? Thank the gods Stryker was above ground; he would make sure this bastard never got his hands on her.

"I see you are beginning to understand." Passio moved closer and pinched Dallin's nipples.

Growling deep in his chest, Dallin stared at the demon, his cat rising to the surface, ready to morph. "She will never love you."

"My guards will break your spine before you shift." The demon grinned. "I need you alive but paralyzed is just as good." Passio bent his head close to Dallin's face. "Perhaps I'll keep you here after all. I can always take Cruz for a trade. He is the spare, isn't he? It would be amusing to know that you are watching me feed on Lailii. Can you imagine seeing her spread her legs for Kaos and me until you grow old and die? Knowing you can never have her . . .

never have any female. Of course, at first she will believe that you and Stryker are here with her."

"How stupid do you think she is?"

The next instant, Stryker stood before him, grinning like a monkey. Dallin took a deep breath; the disgusting scent of violets remained. This was not Stryker, just a facsimile. Gods, the demon could morph into anyone he desired.

"She will believe anything I wish." Passio chuckled softly. "When Kaos and I bite her, she will be in ecstasy. She will give herself willingly to us."

The knot in Dallin's stomach increased. He tried to jump. Pain, sharp and vicious, slammed into his head. His knees buckled. With a groan, he lifted his chin. "So when my father refuses the trade, will you force me to become one of your Army of Lost Souls?"

"No, they are mutants, Dallin, although I'm not surprised a mere mortal couldn't distinguish the difference." Passio chuckled. "My castle is for demi-gods; mutants are held in limbo to rise up when and where I command. You would become my *special* prisoner."

Dallin coughed, and then spat in the demon's face. The guards wrenched his arms back. Pain shot into his spine. The sight of his spittle dripping off Passio's chin was worth the discomfort.

"Take him away." Passio waved his hand.

The guards dragged him down a passageway. From the windows, Dallin stared out at an impressive fortress set against a forbidding sky. They passed a row of doors, walked through a small vestibule, and along another corridor. They met no one. The entire building was eerily silent. The polished wood floors echoed with the sound of their footfalls. The guards' extraordinary strength surprised Dallin. Their grips around his arms cut off the blood supply. If they were all this strong, he had little chance of overpowering them.

They entered a long hall—no, a ballroom with a crystal chandelier. Graphic paintings depicting scenes of brutality lined one wall. To the right, a Gate took up the entire façade. The flashing scenes of a variety of familiar realms displayed on the silver screen caught Dallin's attention. Another wall held an impressive display of swords. A door swung open as they approached. The guards pushed him forward, and he stared down a flight of damp stairs. A rush of warm, putrid air hit him in the face. Without warning, a blow between the shoulders sent the breath rushing from his lungs. Dallin toppled and fell down the steps, hitting the filthy flagstones with a thud. He rolled to his feet and gazed down a line of cages. The dungeon stank of death. Men beaten and broken moaned in despair, their thin bodies chained to the grimy walls. There was no escape.

Lailii's face flashed across his mind. He balled his hands into fists. That damn demon would never take her away from him. She belonged to him, and he would fight to his last breath to save her from this place. Surely, his father would not think to exchange her for him. Then again, Stryker would take her away to safety at the first sign of danger. All he needed to do was to escape this dungeon and get to the Gate without Passio noticing. *Yeah right.*

The guards walked down the stairs behind him, their boots clattering on the wooden steps. Dallin glanced around for an escape route. There was no other way out. With no windows and only one door, the demon had sealed the dungeon from the outside like a huge, concrete coffin. Water dripped down the bloodstained walls, mixing with a river of piss and shit. There was no doubt this was hell. He turned to face the guards, ready to fight. They were gigantic and wore black body armor. He would not stand a chance against them. A pang of fear hit him. They wore leather helms, but no eyes returned his gaze through the slits, only the black holes of empty eye sockets.

A blow to the side of the head sent him to the floor. Blood spilled into his mouth. Dallin grasped one of the guard's feet and tipped the brute over. The man crashed to the floor, sending up a spray of putrid water. A massive hand curled in Dallin's hair, lifting him with ease. Pain sheared through his chest from a boot in the ribs. Gasping for air, he staggered to his feet, fists raised. A cage door creaked open, and one of the men flung him inside. He hit the floor like a rag doll. The door slammed shut behind him, the sound reverberating around the dungeon. Men screamed in terror. Without a sound, the guards turned away and vanished in a puff of swirling black smoke.

Dallin rolled onto all fours and spat the blood from his mouth. He dragged his broken body up and tested the door and bars for weakness. The cells on either side of him were empty. Across the walkway, a beaten and bloody man lifted his head and moaned with despair. Dallin glanced around the cell. Better than the other cages, this one had a small cot with a blanket, a table containing a jug of water, and a plate of bread and cheese. The floor, covered with clean straw, was a stark contrast to the other cells. At least Passio intended to keep him alive. Dallin ground his teeth and shuddered in disgust. He would go out fighting if that bastard believed he would become his sex slave. He sat on the edge of the bed and dropped his head in his hands. *Dear Lady, you said I had the ability to fight demons. Now tell me, how the hell am I going to get out of this mess?*

* * * * *

Banin Mountain.

Stryker followed Cruz toward the fissure, the men fanning out around them, searching the area. "The stick is there between the rocks. Dallin can't be far away."

"He must be unconscious, or he would answer his phone." Cruz frowned. "He usually loses the ability to cloak if he's knocked out. It's a conscious action. I don't think he's here. I hope he didn't get sucked through the damn Gate."

Rubbing his chin, Stryker gazed around. A flat spot in the long grass caught his attention. He walked toward it, noticing the sun reflecting on something.

He fell to his knees and searched the undergrowth. His fingers found Dallin's amulet. Blood pounded in his ears. Deep, agonizing loss slammed into him. He waved on his knees. Choking down grief, he swallowed hard and held the chain high. "Gods, Cruz, take a look at this. Dallin must be dead. He vowed he would never remove this after our joining."

"He's not fucking dead." Cruz bunched his fists on his hips. "He's the Lady's Champion. Do you think She sent us to get Lailii, and then allowed him to die? Get a grip, man." He shook his head. "My guess is the demons dragged him into the Underworld."

Stryker got to his feet. He placed the chain over his head and tucked it into his shirt. He wished he had Cruz's faith. In his heart, he feared Dallin was dead. "Do you think the Lady would let that happen? I don't think so; he must be here somewhere. I have to find him."

"What you have to do is get back to Vane Castle." Cruz met Stryker's gaze. "Go to the Lady's grotto and beg for Her help." He growled. "Don't give me a load of shit about not being worthy to enter the grotto, either. You are Dallin's mate, he is in trouble, and we need the Lady's help."

With a grunt, Stryker turned toward the lines of flybikes at the edge of the clearing. He stopped and turned to Cruz. "Are you going to keep searching?"

"I'm going to call my father and update him on the situation." Cruz frowned. "I'll leave men here whatever his decision. Go."

* * * * *

Vane Castle

Lailii sat on the edge of the cot and stared into the faces of Dallin's brothers. Both were appalled at their father for confining her in the dungeon but could not go against the king's orders. They could only make her comfortable until Dallin returned. Zane, the youngest at eighteen years old, crouched at her feet, trying unsuccessfully to remove the silver from her wrists. She sighed. "They were sealed with a spell. I believe only the smithy can remove them." Lailii met Kaden's gaze. "Are my mates returning home?"

"I can't contact Dallin. He may be having trouble with his phone so close to a demon Gate. And this is not something I wish to discuss with Cruz." Kaden pushed a lock of black hair off his face. "I'll leave immediately and apprise Dallin personally of the situation." He took Lailii's hand. "My father has become unstable in his old age. Try not to worry. Zane will stay by your side until your mates return. I will order a cot for him to sleep in here." He turned to Zane. "Don't leave her side. The door to this cell remains open at all times. I've ordered extra food. I'll be back as soon as possible. If you have trouble with the guards, use your zap."

* * * * *

The king held up his hand to still the guards waiting to pounce on the intruder.

"Who are you, and how in the Lady's name did you breach my security?"

"I am Lord Passio." The man genuflected. "This island belonged to me before your Pride existed." Passio smiled. "I've come to make you an offer for your son. He is safe in my dungeon for the time being."

The King shook his head. "I find that hard to believe."

"Oh, you will believe." Passio touched the hilt of his sword. "I'm sure your son will contact you soon."

"If what you say is true, what do you want?"

"I will trade your son for the Spellweaver residing in your dungeon." Passio lifted his chin. "She obviously is of no worth to you, so your decision is easy."

The king's phone buzzed. He turned his back and spoke to Cruz. His worst fears realized, he closed his Ocular phone and swore colorfully. He spun around and glowered at the strangely dressed man standing before him in the solar. "So you *do* have my son."

"I may be a demon, but I do tell the truth some of the time." Passio smiled. "Do we have a bargain — Prince Dallin in exchange for the lowly Spellweaver? I only require *one* soul to appease my master, Lord Baltor. This is such a small request for your son and heir, don't you think?" He dropped a document on the table. "My time here is limited — make up your mind."

The king ran a hand through his hair. "I only know my son is missing at this point. I have no proof you have him."

"Will this do?" Passio dropped Dallin's gold signet ring into the king's palm. "The royal seal, I believe?"

"What do you want me to do?"

"Have the Spellweaver brought here, sign the contract, and I'll leave your son in a place you can find him." Passio looked at his fingernails. "You have seven minutes."

The king picked up the contract. "What guarantee do I have my son will be returned unharmed?"

"Read the contract." Passio raised a brow. "You can read, I assume?"

With a grimace, the King re-read the document, and then met Passio's gaze. "It says that you require a soul. Do I assume this is the Spellweaver?"

"I need a soul—any soul will do." Passio yawned. "Do we have a bargain?"

This contract will rid me of my problem. The king smiled. He cared less about the damn Spellweaver. He had no problem exchanging her and her bastard cub for his son. He lifted a gold pen from the table and made his mark on the contract. He turned to his squire. "Bring the Spellweaver. Jump her here. I don't have much time."

Lailii panicked the instant the king's squire appeared in her cell. She got to her feet, drawing a blanket around her shoulders against the chill in the dungeon. Without saying a word, the young squire clasped one of her arms. She reached for Zane, her fingers closing around the collar of his jacket. The next second, she found herself in the king's solar with Zane at her side, zap raised. She recognized the dark magyck in the room and turned to face Passio. Her legs trembled. Could this be the old demon everyone feared, this young, handsome man?

"Father, what are you doing?" Zane dropped his zap and stood in front of Lailii. "This cruelty has gone far enough."

"So she has bewitched you as well." The king backhanded his son across the face. "Step away, whelp, she is going with the demon."

"No." Zane stood his ground. "You can't do this."

"He has kidnapped Dallin. She is the trade." The king laughed. "A very poor trade but the contract is signed."

"Yes, and a soul is part of our bargain." Passio gave a throaty laugh and withdrew a sword from a scabbard at his waist. "I chose *your* soul." With one swift movement, he decapitated the king.

Lailii watched the king's body sink to the floor in a sea of crimson. The king's grotesquely twisted lips still moved in the bloody, spinning head. Zane stood open mouthed, his face frozen in a mask of terror. Lailii wanted to scream, but no sound came out of her throat. Passio's long fingers curled around her arm, and she spun into a kaleidoscope of colors.

* * * * *

Underworld.

Dallin paced the confines of the cage. He needed a plan. There was not much to work with, and time was difficult to gauge. The guards had returned sporadically to torture the prisoners. The beasts tied each man to a crucifix and whipped him to unconsciousness. The sickening sounds of the men's cries tore at Dallin's heart. During the beatings, the guards never uttered a sound—not a grunt, nothing. Racking his brain for ideas, Dallin went over the battle with the Army of Loss Souls. The mutants had cried out during the battle and bled like pigs. He concluded that the guards were not mutants as he had suspected but rather conjured beings. He knew the spell used to create slaves. Many Prides used this form of magyck because they detested inequality. He sighed. His father was old school; he expected his subjects to bow and be subservient. At least the king paid his servants well.

The door to the dungeon opened. Men cried out in panic. Passio preceded the guards, holding a red silk cloth over his nose, his eyes dancing with amusement. Dallin reached for the blanket and slung it around his hips. The thought of the man's eyes on his naked body made him sick. His stomach cramped. Perhaps the guards would beat him while Passio watched. In a moment of complete clarity, he decided Passio would never hear a cry of pain from his mouth. *You'll never break me.* His mind flicked back to the first time he went into combat. His grandfather's voice echoed in his memory. *"Show no fear."*

Dallin straightened his shoulders and stood in the center of the cage. He met Passio's gaze. "Is this the best accommodation you can provide? Or haven't you noticed it stinks in here."

"Well, I could have offered you a bargain for more suitable lodging, but alas you won't be staying." Passio moved closer to the cell. "I'm surprised to see you on your feet." Passio waved the silk cloth in front of his face. "You look fine, not even a broken rib or two. I'll have to supervise my guards in the future."

The next second, darkness surrounded Dallin; the moons and stars flashed before his eyes. As he fell, his instinct to morph came too late, and he hit the grass with a thud. He lifted his head and stared into a clear, starlit night, the two moons bright overhead. Naked and without weapons, he morphed into his cat. Through cat's eyes, he made out a forest about a mile away. This place was familiar. He could recognize Banin Mountain rising above the trees in the distance. Watchful for any sign of mutants, he lifted his head and drew in the scents of the night. No stench of the walking dead accosted him; only the heavy aroma of cooking permeated the air. He waited for the prickling sensation over his skin from dark magyck, lifted his head, and felt . . . nothing untoward. Instead, he sensed there were people close by. He bounded into the darkness, keeping to the shadows, his black and white-striped coat camouflage in the moonlight.

He reached the edge of the forest and slinked toward the camp. Groups of men huddled around campfires, eating and speaking in hushed tones. Dallin recognized the scents of the men—*his* men. Cruz sat on a log, eating with gusto from a tin plate.

Dallin morphed and strode toward him. "Where's Stryker?"

"Where the fuck have you been?" Cruz jumped to his feet, the plate spilling unheeded to the ground. "You look like hell."

"Maybe because I've been to hell and back. Answer the question."

"He's on his way back to the castle. He thinks you're dead." Cruz scratched his cheek. "I told him to go see the Lady and ask for help."

Dallin dragged a hand through his hair. "I need clothes. Where did you put my backpack?"

"It's in my tent." Cruz pointed behind him. "I'll get you some food."

"Don't bother; I don't have time. I need to fill you in on the situation"

Dallin headed for the tent with Cruz on his heels. He sat on the cot and dragged clothes from his backpack. "Passio took me into the Underworld to trade for Lailii. If I'm here, our father traded her for me." He pulled on his pants. "I can't save her on my own. The demon guards are monsters."

"How can you possibly enter the Underworld? We've sealed all the Gates." Cruz rubbed his chin. "That damn fissure is useless; it could lead to Baltor himself."

With a growl, Dallin pulled on his boots and stood fully dressed. "Passio lives in a fortress, but inside is a Gate. I recognized some of the scenes. One is on top of Devil's Peak."

"On Demon Island? I find that hard to believe." Cruz scratched his head. "A demon Gate in our own backyard and we didn't notice? You have to be mistaken."

"It's on the east side. I could see Vane Castle in the distance."

"That's sheer rock; it's impossible to get there, even on a flybike." Cruz frowned. "There's no place to land. How do expect to get an army up there?"

Dallin strode from the tent. "I have no idea. Give me your phone; I'll contact Stryker."

"The phones have been out for the past couple of hours." Cruz took the phone from his pocket and handed it to him. "Maybe the damn thing will work now you're back."

He took the phone and met Cruz's gaze. "Get the troops moving. I must get home without delay. My only hope is to consult with the Lady."

The phone buzzed. Dallin flipped it open, and Zane's hologram appeared. Tears streaked the young man's face. "Dallin? Thank the gods. I've tried to reach you for hours. F-father is d-dead."

Dallin stared at his brother's hologram in disbelief. He could hear Cruz's sharp intake of breath at his side. "What happened? Take it slow."

"Everything has gone to h-hell." Zane buried his face in his hands.

"I can't help if you don't tell me what's happened." Dallin sighed. If he must coax the story from his brother, he would. He lowered his voice. "When did you get back with Kaden?"

"About four hours ago. Peter came to us frantic because father had locked Lailii in the dungeon." Zane met Dallin's gaze. "He silvered her."

Fear curled in Dallin's belly. "He what?"

"I tried to remove the silver, but it had a binding spell on it. Kaden couldn't reach you by phone and left straight away to let you know what was happening." Zane drew a shuddering breath. "Next thing I know, I'm in the s-solar with Lailii, and a demon is standing there. He made a trade with father. He wanted Lailii in exchange for you." Zane covered his eyes. "The d-demon cut off f-father's h-head and vanished with Lailii."

Biting back grief, Dallin stared at his brother's hologram in disbelief. Dear Lady, the demon had Lailii. Pain stabbed his chest. *Oh, little one, I should never have left you alone.* How could his father have done such a thing? Why did the demon kill him? He had to get home and beg the Lady for help. "I'm leaving now. Contact Kaden, and tell him to turn back. I'm on the way. Tell Stryker. In my estimation, he should be landing shortly."

He shut the phone and stared into the darkness. Bone-deep grief, not for his father but for Lailii, tore at his heart. Gods, he had promised the Lady to protect her from Passio, and he might have just as well handed her over to him. Bile rose in his throat. His sweet Lailii had suffered by his own flesh and blood. He spat on the ground. "Damn you to hell, Father."

Chapter Ten

Underworld

Lailii pulled the blanket around her and glared at Passio. "Y-you killed the king." She tried to push the gruesome images from her mind. With the thought of protecting her cub, she straightened her back. She would not show fear. Drawing a deep breath, she attempted to control the sobs in her throat. "W-what do you want with me?"

She stared at the man dressed in a light blue silk jacket with white lace falling over his hands. His matching pants ended at the knee in white stockings, his feet pushed into blue silk slippers with white bows. The man looked less like a demon than anyone she had ever seen—no mutant blood ran in his veins. Yet he killed with no remorse. With an evil grin, Passio glanced at her wrists and gave a low chuckle. The silver bands vanished. Lailii tried to pull her magyck around her, but her powers were weak from the protective spell around her cub.

"Kaos, come and see my prize." Passio spoke to an empty space beside Lailii.

The air shimmered. A twirl of white smoke seeped from the floorboards, rising up and forming a ghostly shape.

"Do you want to scare the girl?" Passio frowned.

The ghost became whole. Lailii blinked. This man had red, flowing hair and emerald green eyes. He dressed similar to Passio, but his choice in silk was yellow. He waved a lace handkerchief at Lailii and winked salaciously.

"I am Kaos, sweet temptress." He inclined his head. "What may I call you?"

Lailii swallowed hard. These were demons, these angelic-looking boys. Was this some kind of sick joke? She trembled. Her fingers gripped the edge of the blanket. These simpering males were going to kill her. The thick scent of violets overwhelmed her, and she covered her mouth. "I think I'm going to vomit."

"That's a bit long." Kaos rubbed his chin. "How about we shorten it to *vomit*?"

"She means she's going to puke." Passio growled. "We'd better take her to her room."

The demons gave jumping an entirely new meaning. Freezing air rammed her body; colors rushed around her. Lailii squeezed her eyes shut and pressed her hand on her stomach. The awful perfume did not leave, and she opened her eyes again to see Passio standing in front of her. Kaos, with a smug grin on his face, leaned casually against the doorframe. They were in a large bedroom. The room had a dresser, a bed, and little else.

"I think you should rest. I will arrange refreshments for you." Passio waved her to the bed.

Unable to flee, Lailii sank down on the edge of the mattress. She bit her bottom lip. What did they want from her—goddess, not her cub? Passio hovered protectively close to her. She lifted her gaze to stare at his handsome face. "Why am I here?"

"All I want is to share a little of your blood." Passio sat beside her. "I am not a monster. I don't intent to bind you in silver or restrict your powers."

With a shudder, Lailii stared at the floor. "My blood? Why would a demon want my blood?"

"Demon is such a harsh word, don't you think?" Passio waved a hand. "Demigod is the correct name for us."

Fallen angels, those beings so evil the Great One banished them to the Underworld? This creature sitting beside her with the simpering voice could not possibly be the great Lord Passio— right hand man of

243

the demon, Baltor? Lailii's head ached. This must be a dream; but no, not even her imagination could possibly create the king's bloody murder.

"She finds us confusing." Kaos glided across the room. "You expected horned beasts, and we disappointed you."

Lailii met Kaos' gaze. The demon's eyes changed from green to red and back. She swallowed hard. "Why do you want my blood?"

"To enhance our powers with your own, sweet lady. Your blood will allow us a little time in the sunshine." Kaos smiled. "Surely, you wouldn't deny us a break away from this place to redeem ourselves?" He touched Lailii's face. "Is it not your goddess's way to forgive?"

Pulling her head away to avoid the demon's cold fingers, Lailii gasped. He had touched her through her magyck as if no barrier existed. She shuddered, fear crawling up her spine. "She won't forgive you for kidnapping me. I belong to her champion. You fall afoul of the gods by taking me away from my mates."

"Your mates are here." Passio reached for her hand. "I will allow them to call on you, but each visit must be paid for in blood."

Lailii shuddered. "They would never allow this to happen."

"They remain alive so long as you comply with my wishes." Passio frowned. "We do not want to hurt you. In time, you will love us."

Remain alive? Had the demon kidnapped Dallin and Stryker too? Her cub was better off dead than born in the Underworld to the mercy of these blood-sucking fiends. They all were. Lailii lifted her chin. "I will never love you, and I know in my heart, my mates would rather die than let me submit to you. We have a sacred bond. You may as well kill us all now, for I will be useless to you. My magyck will soon fade. I need sunshine, love, and happiness. There is none of this in hell."

"Lailii, you underestimate me." Passio chuckled. "I know you recharge your powers with sex. I'll allow you that enjoyment to regenerate your powers. By the time your mates grow old and die, you will see the benefit of having two virile demigods to pleasure you." He drummed his fingers on the satin bedcover. "Now, do you agree to my terms, a little of your blood for an afternoon of passion and the knowledge your mates are safe and well?" He met her gaze his eyes blood red. "Or would you prefer I become the demon you despise. I'll take you into the dungeon and slit your eyelids to make you watch while I peel the flesh from your mates." He smiled. "I will enjoy listening to their screams." He lifted her chin. "Do you know how many days it takes for a man to die without skin?"

The room spun. Lailii coughed, and then spewed vomit over Passio's satin pumps. The demon swore colorfully and fled the room. Kaos' cold hands lifted her feet and lay her on the bed. He wiped her face efficiently and sat beside her. Lailii covered her mouth. Her head throbbed. She turned her face away and ignored the demon.

"Drink this water." Kaos tipped her head toward him and pressed a glass to her lips. "Rest now; in the morning you will see things clearer."

"I want to see my mates."

"I will bring Dallin to you, but only for a few minutes. I'm sure he will tell you to agree to the terms." Kaos got to his feet. "Or you can always try negotiation."

Lailii bit her bottom lip. This had to be a trick. "Negotiation?"

"Yes, set the term of your stay with us." Kaos shrugged. "I'm sure Passio will agree if you give us your complete obedience."

Her gaze followed Kaos to the door. A few minutes later, the door opened and Dallin strode into the room with a broad grin. How strange her mate would think this situation jovial. Dallin sat on the bed and raised one perfect brow. Lailii inhaled to capture his unique scent. She grimaced at the sickly odor accosting her nose. Her hands came up to press against his chest — this was not Dallin. What should she do? Play the game and see what happened? Should she run around the room screaming? Blood pounded in her ears; her cub began to kick hard. Did the babe recognize the deception? *I must survive.* She lifted her mouth to accept the doppelganger's kiss. Cold, hard lips brushed against her mouth, and the taste of violets pushed into her throat. She gagged and turned her head away. "I'm sorry; I'm unwell."

"It's okay." The fake Dallin sat up and took her hands. "I think Lord Passio only requires your blood for a month, then there's a good chance he'll let us all go."

Lord Passio? Another mistake. Dallin would never call a demon 'lord'. Who is this man? "So you would like me to comply? You want me to allow Passio and Kaos to suck my blood?"

"Yes, and Stryker and I will visit you every day." Dallin smiled. "That would be nice, wouldn't it?"

Nice? She could not imagine Dallin using that word with regard to sex either. She had little choice. She needed to boost her powers to keep her cub safe. Seeing copies of her mates would help. How long could she avoid sex? She grimaced at the thought of intimacy with these cold creatures. How would she survive without seeing the sun and nature's beauty? She turned to the fake Dallin. "You know, sweet pea, I have to recharge my powers with nature. How does Passio plan to do this?"

"I love it when you call me that." Dallin beamed. "I'll ask him straight away. You have a sleep, and I'll be back with Stryker later."

Lailii watched him go. Once the door shut behind him, she shook her head. What a fool; imagine a warrior prince like Dallin allowing her to call him *sweet pea. Lady's blood.* She threw her feet over the edge of the bed and noticed to her amazement the puddle of vomit had disappeared. She walked to the window and stared into the gloom. The black castle loomed beneath the window, guards patrolled the walkways, and huge, bat-like creatures swooped or clung to the crenellations. *Gods, Terravampires – I thought they were a myth.* In the distance, high mountains, black and rugged, rose against a turbulent sky. Lightening scored the darkness, showing glimpses of endless peaks.

Folding her arms across her stomach, she rested her forehead against the pane. She had her powers; there must be a spell she could weave to incapacitate a demon. The last few days, her cat had bumped against her conscience, waiting to emerge after the birth of her cub. Therefore, it made perfect sense to assume the cat's Pride magyck already flowed in her veins, waiting for her command. She had the knowledge of ancient incantations, and the ability to kill. She was a Spellweaver, and this is what she trained for all those long years at the Tark. She turned and gazed around the room. Her head ached. Walking slowly, she returned to the bed and lay down. Spells spun through her mind, tumbling her into an enchanted dreamscape.

* * * * *

Demon Island

Stryker landed the flybike beside the gate to the Lady's grotto. He slid off the bike and paced up and down in an effort to collect his thoughts. He had never addressed the Lady in this manner, and the thought of actually standing before his goddess scared the hell out of him. With one hand clasped around Dallin's amulet, he opened the gate and marched into the grotto. A welcoming glow surrounded the interior of the building. The scent of roses filled the night air. He stopped inside the small vestibule and gazed at the bowl of water. Gods, what did he have to do? Drink it? Wash in it? He searched his mind and could not come up with a damn thing. He scooped up the water with his hands and drank a little, splashing the rest over his face. He wiped his hands on his jeans, and then walked through the swirling portal.

Peace surrounded him, and he fell to his knees in the center of the room. He bowed his head. "Dear Lady, unworthy as I am to be in this holy place, I've come to ask your help. Dallin is lost. I think Passio has killed him. I don't know what to do."

The hairs on his nape stood up. His cat shrank in fear. A soft whisper echoed in his head. "*Open your eyes.*"

Stryker's eyes flew open. The shimmery image of a woman sat cross-legged on the floor before him. She smiled sweetly and tossed moonbeam curls over her shoulder. He opened his mouth to speak, and then shut it again with a snap.

"*Don't fear me; I am your goddess.*" She inclined her head. "*You must have faith, Stryker, my champion lives. He is returning to the castle.*"

Stryker grinned. "Thank you."

"*Not so my daughter, Lailii; she is imprisoned by the demon, Passio.*" Her face grew sad. "*I cannot enter the Underworld to save her, nor can you. Once inside, there is no escape for us."* She got to her feet and began to pace the room. *"The Great One allows me only one champion. Dallin must go alone and fight the demon. Bring him here in the morning. I must have time to beg my father for a small indulgence. Use your talent to contact Lailii; make plans for escape."*

Stryker looked at the goddess in disbelief. Passio had Lailii. How could this have happened? Grief hit him like a sledgehammer. He fought words past the lump in his throat. "Will Lailii survive? What about our cub?"

"For now, Lailii surrounds your son with magyck so strong even the demons have not detected his presence. She knows nothing of her heritage. When she was born half-mortal, I locked pure, white magyck deep inside her. It took your bonding to release her goddess power. She will have the knowledge to defeat the demon, but Dallin is the only one capable of bringing her back through the Gate. The innocent cub she carries will prevent the demon magyck no matter what poison they try to inject into her."

"And if Dallin fails?"

"He will become Passio's toy, and Lailii and your son will remain in the Underworld for eternity."

* * * * *

Midnight struck, the old clock in the great hall counting down the hour. Dallin shouted for the servants to feed his starving battalion and ran up the stairs to his parents' chambers. He brushed past the guards and threw open the door. His mother was on her knees before the king's chair, sobbing into the cushion. He moved to her side. "Mother."

"The king is dead, all hail the king." The queen lifted her tear-streaked face. "Are you satisfied now? Your little whore has killed your father."

Dallin's hands balled into fists at his sides. Not even the death of her mate would soften his mother's frozen heart. "Father sent my queen to the Underworld. He imprisoned her and had her bound in silver. Do you know why he would do such a thing?"

"He wanted to make sure you never damaged our bloodline." The queen sobbed. "You live your life with a Talynx, then chose an ancient Spellweaver— you might as well have mated a Neanderthal." She dashed away the tears. "He wanted to burn her the moment you left the castle."

Rubbing his neck, Dallin gazed helplessly at his mother. How could she condone such treatment? "Mother, couldn't you see the man was deranged?"

"*He was my mate.*" The queen staggered to her feet. She slapped Dallin's face, then leaned heavily against the chair and glared at her son. "You will *never* be the king he was. You are weak— I should have drowned you at birth. I should have killed all of you. You don't deserve to live." She sank into a chair. "If you bring that girl and her bastard cub into my castle, I'll destroy them both too. Go away; I can't stand to look at you."

With a shake of his head, Dallin turned to the door. The king's servants hovered in the corridor. "Pack up my mother's belongings; she will be moving to the summer palace first thing in the morning." He turned to his mother. "Well, now you won't have to look at us ever again. Feel free to take your staff with you, Mother. They've become as twisted as you over the years." He strode from the room.

In the hallway, he stopped and pressed both hands against the wall. *Lady help me. I am king, and my queen is trapped in the Underworld.* He must address his people to assure his loyal subjects of his ability to rule with compassion and strength. They would be living in fear of a demon attack. They needed their king — and he needed to rescue his mate. He rested his forehead against the cold stone. Lailii was his first priority.

Gods only knew where Stryker was. His head spun with fatigue; he could not think straight. His cat reminded him that he needed to eat. He sighed and jumped to the great hall. To his surprise, the entire gathering stood on his appearance. He gazed around at the bent heads and prostrated servants. He lifted his chin. "From this day forth, all men are equal. No man will lie at my feet, and a bow is all that I require for courtesy. Those of you who wish to leave the castle may do so. Those who wish to serve me of their own free will may stay. I offer you what any employer offers his staff: good pay with time off and my gratitude."

Applause broke out, along with cries of 'long live the king'. Dallin straightened his weary shoulders and met the gazes of his people. He would speak to his brothers and delegate responsibility for the running of the empire in his absence — or death. "My queen was taken to the Underworld by the demon Passio."

Cries of disbelief echoed through the hall. Women fell to their knees, pleading with the Lady for help. Dallin held up his hand for silence. "I am the Lady's Champion; you have my word as your king, my mate will be returned."

Amongst the cheers and well wishes, Dallin strode to the head of the table. He sank into his father's chair and waited for his squire to fill his plate. Before he took his first bite, Stryker walked stiffly into the great hall. The man looked bone weary, and his hair stood out in all directions. He let out a long groan and slumped into the chair beside Dallin. Meeting his lover's gaze, Dallin squeezed Stryker's hand under the table. "Passio's got Lailii."

"I know; I went to see the Lady. Then when I left the grotto, Zane filled me in by phone. I can't believe this; it's a fucking nightmare." Stryker downed a full goblet of Miza, then refilled his glass. "Best we eat. After, we'll go up to our room to discuss what the goddess told me."

Dallin dropped Stryker's hand and rubbed both palms over his face. "I'm worried— what if the demon has hurt Lailii and she loses our cub?"

"You look like you've been dropped off a flybike." Stryker grimaced. "How did you survive the Underworld?"

"Dunno. Passio let me go when he swapped me for Lailii." He groaned. "*Lailii*, gods, Stryker, she hasn't got a chance down there. They're not what I imagined, but they have more power in their pinky finger than our entire Pride." He stared into the distance. "Fuck, for the first time in my life, I don't know what to do." Dallin met Stryker's gaze." The Underworld is like nothing I've ever faced before. Not the fire and brimstone I expected – the demons look almost normal, but they're psychopaths. They feed on fear and pain." His hands closed into fists, and he banged on the table. "I felt defenseless and weak. The guards have this superhuman strength, and when I tried magyck, my head almost exploded. I'm guessing the zaps won't work either." He held his head in his hands and moaned. "I have to work out some brilliant tactic to beat them, and then try and find a way back into the Underworld without being detected."

"Eat. The Lady is working on a plan." Stryker accepted the plate of food from a servant and began to eat. "You'll need your strength. The goddess wants to see you first thing in the morning."

With a shrug, Dallin forked up some food. His lover was right. He must be strong to meet this challenge. Lailii's life depended on it. "Oh, I bet the Lady's real pleased with me. She gave me one specific thing to do. *Take care of Lailii.* What do I do? I lose her in under a month."

"I don't think the demon wants to kill her, or he would have done it by now." Stryker's brow furrowed. "I believe Passio wants her for her powers. This being the case, he'll need to keep her happy, or she won't have any magyck for him to steal. This at least gives us a little time."

"How will he extract her magyck?" Dallin chewed slowly. "She can't just hand it to him. Gods, my stomach is in knots just thinking of her in that place. I feel so fucking useless." He reached for his wine and drank, then placed the goblet back on the table. "I fear our cub will not survive such terror. We will be lucky to get her out of there alive. If Passio knows she is immortal, he'll know how to kill her too. The bastard will do it out of spite."

"We have a son." Stryker whispered. "The Lady said our *son* was safe."

Tears pricked the backs of Dallin's eyes. *A son he would never see.* He dashed his knuckles over his cheeks and drew a deep breath. He grabbed Stryker by the back of the neck, drew him close, and kissed him hard. Stryker's large hand closed over Dallin's thigh and met Dallin's kiss with urgent passion. His body responded, his cock pressing hard against the front of his pants. Reluctantly, Dallin pulled away and met his mate's eyes. "*Promise* me, if you have to make the decision to save Lailii or me, you choose her and our son."

"Lady willing, I'll never have to make that decision. But you have my word." Stryker smiled thinly. "Although I don't think Cruz would agree. He doesn't want to be king."

Dallin snorted. He ran the pad of his thumb across Stryker's bottom lip. "He won't be. On my death, my son will become king, and as my mate, you will make it so."

"Oh yeah." Stryker lifted Dallin's gold amulet from under his shirt. "This belongs to you. I found it near the demon fissure."

Thank the gods. Dallin gazed into Stryker's clear green eyes. How he loved the man. In all the confusion and pain, his lover stood beside him like a rock. "You keep it safe for me until I return." He brushed Stryker's lips with a kiss. "I won't be able to sleep worrying about Lailii. I need you so bad. I want to take the sweet memory of our love with me into the Underworld — my shield against the horror."

Chapter Eleven

Later, in Dallin's bedchamber, Stryker shrugged out of his clothes, and then turned to gaze at the prince. Purple bruises covered the man's body. "Morph. You need to heal those bruises. You'll need to be in shape to fight Passio."

The air shimmered around Dallin, and a white tiger appeared. The next instant, Dallin stood before him again, in perfect health. Stryker smiled and moved closer. He ran both hands down Dallin's muscular arms. "I think you deserve to relax in the hot tub, and then perhaps have a nice massage."

"Sounds good. I'll put the Loop out. I don't want her attacking you again when we make love." Dallin moved to the bed, scooped the sleeping beast up in one hand, and walked to the door. "Why don't you make sure that tub is nice and hot?"

Stryker strolled into the bathroom. He placed one finger in the water to heat it with magyck, and then slipped into the bubbling water. Dallin joined him, his muscular body gleaming in the water. With one stride, Stryker closed the distance between them. Splashing water over the edge of the hot tub, he straddled Dallin's thighs and sank his fingers into the man's damp hair. His mouth closed over his lover's full lips; his tongue fought and gained entrance. Dallin's long fingers dug in his hips, lifting him with urgency. The mushroom head of the man's cock found Stryker's hole and thrust home. So full and hot, Stryker moaned into Dallin's mouth. Without complaint, Stryker let Dallin take charge. The man thrust upward, sending great waves crashing over the edge of the tub. Long, sizzling shivers of desire curled in his belly. He kissed Dallin hard, dragging his head closer. He drank in his flavor, branding it in his memory forever. His lover drove in deep, trembled, and came. Hot jets of cum filled his ass. Stryker sighed. He would take his lover long and slow in bed – give him a night to remember. Dallin pulled his head away, his lips swollen from the kiss. Stryker met his passionate gaze. "I love you."

"I love you, too."

After half an hour of soaking, Dallin climbed from the tub and dried off on a white, fluffy towel. Stryker had explained his visit to the Lady. Dallin headed toward the bed to find Stryker had placed an assortment of oils on the nightstand.

"Sandalwood, I think. Lie on your stomach." Stryker poured oil into the palm of his hand.

Dallin climbed onto the bed and sighed. He enjoyed the way Stryker's hands moved across his skin. He tried to concentrate on the plan to rescue Lailii. Fear for her safety constantly pushed logical thought from his mind. "Okay, what do we have so far? I'll dress like a guard. That's easy enough; they wear black and a leather helm. Are you sure you can Dreamwalk in Lailii's dreams?"

"Yes, and your dreams too, with any luck. I'll try to link us." Stryker massaged oil into Dallin's buttocks. "At least she'll know we're coming for her. It's a shame I can't give her the Lady's plans." He sighed. "Try to stop worrying; there's nothing more you can do tonight until we go to bed."

"I don't think I'll sleep tonight."

"You must, or I can't Dreamwalk in your dreams." Stryker kissed a path down Dallin's back. "Let me relax you."

With a groan, Dallin opened his legs to allow Stryker access to his ass. He loved the way Stryker used his fingers to tease him. The small circles of his lover's thumb made Dallin's cock rock hard. "Make sure you ask her exactly where she is. I'm guessing

Passio has her in a room near the ballroom. I saw a row of doors in a hallway close by."

"Turn over." Stryker wiped his hands on a towel. "Bring those knees up." He positioned himself between Dallin's knees.

A shudder of anticipation fluttered Dallin's stomach. He loved this dominant side of Stryker. Hell, he loved the man full stop. He lay back and met Stryker's determined gaze.

Stryker crawled up Dallin's body, lapping his tongue across sculpted muscle. He nibbled and suckled the man's flat nipples, then moved to suck the throbbing vein in his neck. The overpowering desire to bite hit him like a sledgehammer. His venom sacs filled, and his face ached. This should not be happening. He dragged his attention away from Dallin's neck and kissed a path down his belly. Dallin's cock stood away from his groin, the top moist with pre-cum. He groaned and bent to lick the sticky tip. Dallin's unique flavor exploded over his tongue.

He drew the heavy shaft into his mouth and savored the feel of the silken skin across his tongue.

"I want you inside me." Dallin groaned, his fingers fisting in Stryker's hair.

The desire to fuck his lover and bite his tender, fragrant skin surged through Stryker in an uncontrollable rage. His cat roared. Stryker reared up and plunged forward, taking Dallin's tight star in one hot slide. So damn tight, Dallin's heat surrounded him. He rode him like a mad man, the short sighs of encouragement from Dallin driving him deeper, harder. Stryker gazed into his lover's smoldering eyes and inhaled his intoxicating scent. Magyck crackled in the air between them. Sizzling tremors of exquisite delight started in his balls and shot down his legs. Molten lava careened out of control and climbed up his shaft. He drove in deep and fell forward, his fangs burying in the soft flesh of Dallin's throat. As the man's blood filled his mouth, Stryker came in a shuddering rush. Beneath him, Dallin trembled and covered them both with hot spurts of cum.

Long seconds passed. They lay panting, wrapped in each other's arms. Stryker lifted his head to meet Dallin's gaze. "Was that something to remember me by?"

"Oh . . . yeah. You are irresistible when you lose control. Though I never thought you would bite me. Fuck—I loved it." Dallin gave him a crooked smile. "I like the bad boy side of you."

Stryker cupped Dallin's face in his hands. "Come back to me, and I'll be bad any time you want." He brushed his mouth over Dallin's lips. "Let's take a shower and get some sleep. I have some Dreamwalking to do."

* * * * *

Underworld

Lailii awoke and scrambled up until her back pressed against the headboard. She trembled at the sight of Passio and Kaos standing practically naked beside the bed. Only silk loincloths covered their sex. They sat down each side of her, the sickly fragrance of violets seeping into the air. She muttered spells under her breath, but every incantation she tried bounced off the men. She met Passio's meaningful gaze. The demon's intent showed clearly in his expression. "Please, don't do this. My magyck will die if you rape me."

"Rape you?" Passio waved a hand dismissively. "When you come to us, it will be willingly." He lifted her hand and licked a path across her wrist. "I'm here for payment for Dallin's visit."

With her heart threatening to burst through her chest, Lailii kicked out at the demons. Passio held her firmly in his ice-cold grip. Kaos grinned maniacally and took her other arm. She glared at him. "Payment? That wasn't Dallin, and you know it."

"You kissed him. Now we demand payment. Just a few drops of blood will be sufficient." Kaos kissed the underside of her wrist. "From here — the veins in your neck are tainted by cat."

You are disgusting creatures. Lailii shuddered. There must be a way to appease the demons. She needed more time to think. There must be a spell that would work—a poison, perhaps? Could she taint her own blood without killing her cub? It would take the purest white magyck. Would they allow her to recharge her powers? She lifted her chin and gazed into Passio's red eyes. "I want your word, and I know you must keep a bargain. If I agree to this, you will promise never to rape me, not you or Kaos or anyone else in this gods forsaken place." She glanced from one to the other. "You do understand taking blood may kill me when my powers are so low? I cannot sustain a power drain. What do you have to recharge my magyck? If you think to fool me with visits from false mates, you may think again."

"I agree to your terms, sweet lady. Tonight, we will take but a morsel. You cannot die from our bloodletting, but your powers will indeed fail." Passio smiled benevolently. "I will escort you to the Gate. You may feast your eyes on the panoramic vistas.

Such beauty will boost your powers. Of course, for this indulgence, I will take another sip of blood. Do we have an agreement?"

I have no choice if I want to live. Lailii nodded. "Very well, but I'll agree if you promise to take only a little of my blood each time."

"As you wish." Passio helped her from the bed and led her to the door. "As you are weak, we shall walk the few steps to the Gate."

They walked along a long passageway. If she intended to sneak about this place looking for an escape, she must be able to find her way back to her room. She counted the doors. Her room was the fourth from the vestibule. They reached a ballroom, and Passio led her toward a massive Gate. The desire to fling herself through the first scene deserted her the second she noticed the guards. At least six of the brutes stood in the shadows, dark, menacing sentries, evil to the core. She shivered. So much dark magyck flowed through this room, the hairs on her nape stood bolt upright. She concentrated on the Gate and the many scenes flashing by. When she saw Vane Castle far in the distance, its windows ablaze with light, her heart gave a small lurch. Power flowed into her at the knowledge her mates were just a step away.

Out of the corner of her eye, she noticed swirls of mist. The room grew cold, and the smell of violets increased tenfold. The awful sensation of someone watching her crept into her consciousness. She glanced around. A crowd of ghostly shadows moved closer. Translucent faces slid in and out of focus. In places, the air shimmered, and people materialized, all wearing different costumes from all times in history. She swallowed hard. The demons had fangs and eyes as red as blood. Their unwavering attention focused entirely on her.

"Continue to watch the Gate, dear one." Passio turned her toward the Gate. "My friends are only curious. I only allow them to come out at night. You are a refreshing change from watching the floggings in the dungeon."

Don't let them distract you. Lailii concentrated on the scenes. She opened her mind and absorbed as much power as possible. In a single thought, she boosted the spell around her cub and turned to Passio. "I will need to return in the daylight. There is little I can gain from the night."

"Go back to your rooms." Passio addressed the crowd. "When Lailii is ready to entertain you, I will call for you." He took Lailii's elbow. "You glow so charmingly when you recharge. Come, I'll send you back to your chamber."

In an instant, Lailii arrived in her room. Passio lifted her onto the bed, and both men sat beside her, taking hold of her wrists like before. The demons dropped their fangs and bit into her wrists simultaneously. Pain seared up her arms. Lailii cried out. They bit down hard, tearing through her flesh and entering her veins. Bile rushed into her mouth. Passio lifted his head, pushing a strand of fair hair from his face. Blood dripped from the corner of his mouth and ran down his hairless chest to drip off one flat nipple.

"Your blood intoxicates." Passio pulled Kaos up by his hair. "Enough. I am drunk with the euphoria of white magyck."

Lailii gaped at the open holes in her wrists and pulled her throbbing arms to her chest. The demons swayed, giggling and pointing at each other. Kaos climbed awkwardly across the bed and kissed Passio, then began to lick the trail of blood running down the demon's chest. Kaos grunted like a pig and suckled on Passio's small, brown nipple. Passio grasped his friend's head and forced him downward. Kaos obediently bent his head to swallow his master's swollen shaft. Passio grinned sheepishly at Lailii. She turned her head away and closed her eyes, too weak to escape the noise of the demons' debauchery.

Sometime later, Passio began to laugh. The sound of his merriment faded away. The room became freezing cold. Lailii opened her eyes. Both demons had vanished. She slid under the blankets and examined her wrists. Not a mark remained. Her heart rate began to return to normal. She must escape this hell. Her only chance would be to drug the demons. She could do this. With a sigh, she lay back and began to weave a spell.

> *When demons seek my blood,*
> *Release a potent drug,*
> *Fueled by magyck so white,*
> *No demon may fight.*
> *Sleep will come, with no harm to my little one.*
> *As so I say, so mote it be.*

In the morning, once the Gate's vistas recharged her powers, she would allow the demons to feed. The spell would put them to sleep. Then she would make her escape. She may be able to reach the portal. If she ran toward the Gate, the guards may not catch her. Gods, she wished Dallin had taught her how to jump. She closed her eyes and allowed sleep to come.

She walked into the sunshine and rested her hand on Argos. The wind brushed her hair, and the sweet scent of roses filled the air.

"There you are." Stryker stepped into the sunlight and touched her face. "Dallin is here too. I'm in your dreamscape, sweetheart."

Lailii turned to see Dallin walking toward her. She opened her arms, and he pulled her close to his hard body. She sighed. "You feel so real."

"We know you are with Passio, little one." Dallin lifted her chin. "I'm coming to get you. The Lady has a plan."

"Where are you?" Stryker slid his arm around her waist. "Dallin knows the castle."

So warm, she wanted to snuggle into the safe cocoon of her mates' love. With a sigh, she met Stryker's green gaze. "I'm in the fourth room from the vestibule, not far from the Gate room. There are others here – ghosts or apparitions – but Passio only allows them to appear at night. Passio has a second, a demon he calls Kaos. I've weaved a spell; when they drink my blood again, they'll fall asleep.

"When they drink again? Gods, little one, are they draining your blood?" Dallin cursed colorfully.

"What about our cub? The poison may kill him." Stryker said.

"He is safe, bound in an impenetrable spell. They took only a little blood from my wrists. Don't worry; it's nothing. In the morning, I'll regenerate my powers. They'll drink again and fall asleep."

"Delay for as long as you can. Insist on eating — anything. I'll go to the Lady at first light and seek her guidance." Dallin kissed her. "I will come for you — I promise." He dropped his arms and disappeared.

Lailii turned to Stryker and kissed him. "I wish we could communicate like this all the time."

"Sleep now, knowing we are on our way." Stryker stepped away and faded into the shadows.

Chapter Twelve

Dallin rolled out of bed. The sound of water running led him to the shower. He stepped into the cubicle behind Stryker and let the hot water run down his body. "You should have waked me."

"I did. You said you were awake. I've ordered breakfast, and don't tell me you can't eat. You know the rules, king, or no king. You *will* eat before you go into combat." Stryker stepped from the shower and shook his hair, sending water spraying in all directions. He gave Dallin a long, hot look. "I can't

279

live without you. Lailii and me, we need you to complete us. Promise me you'll come back."

"Trust me; I'm not planning on staying voluntarily." Dallin grimaced. "How about you promising me you won't leave me in hell? I don't want to end up Passio's ass slave."

"I'll get you out." Stryker reached for a towel. "Have I ever let you down?"

Dallin turned off the water using magyck and stared at Stryker. The man always had his back in battle. He could trust him with his life, but this was different. Gods, he was scared, terrified of failing. The thought of going into the Underworld filled him with dread. Lailii's sweet face invaded his thoughts. He swallowed hard. For the first time, his path was clear. He would bring her out of the Underworld. *Whatever it takes, little one, whatever it takes.*

He looked at Stryker, realizing the man still waited for his answer. "No, you have never let me down."

* * * * *

One hour later, the sun crept above the horizon. Dallin walked purposefully toward the Lady's grotto, Buzz perched on his shoulder. He had no idea why the Loop had insisted on accompanying him. Stryker and his brothers fell in step beside him, the early morning mist swirling around their legs with every stride. They had his orders and all waited to discover what the Lady had planned. Their boots crunched on the gravel pathway to the Lady's grotto. Dallin paused at the gate and turned to his brothers. "I will go inside with Stryker."

The princes said nothing in reply. Dallin drew a deep breath and moved into the vestibule. He washed his hands and waited until Stryker did likewise. They stepped through the swirling blue portal together. Stryker gasped something unintelligible and dropped to his knees. The Loop jumped from Dallin's shoulder and went straight to the shimmering figure of the Lady. Speechless, Dallin fell to his knees beside his lover.

"The Great One, recognizing our dilemma, has granted me a few considerations." The Lady opened her arms. *"There is no way for a mortal to enter the Gate to the Underworld unless escorted by a demon. Therefore, I give you a choice. Immortality will gain you entrance, but if you fail, you will suffer an eternity of misery. If you succeed, you have my daughter for all time."* She began to pace. *"Secondly, you cannot enter directly into Passio's castle; the gate is heavily guarded. You will have to breach the stronghold. As the Great One built the castle, he designed passageways for this purpose. One lies beneath the rear of the fourth tower."* She stopped pacing and gazed down at Dallin. *"The Loop is your transport. At your command, she will become the fiercest dragon or a Terravampire. The latter will allow you to enter the Underworld undetected. Get inside the castle, rescue my daughter, and leave by the Gate. The Loop will carry you from the mountain to safety. Stryker will wait at the portal, for the demon has Gates into*

many times in history. Do not move through the Gate until you see Stryker on the other side."

Dallin's blood pounded in his ears. He had so many questions. Drawing a steadying breath, he met the Lady's gaze. "How will I fight? The guards are powerful, and the use of my magyck causes great pain. What weapon may I carry to destroy Passio? And what of the other wretched souls trapped in the dungeons?"

"I will weep for their lost souls. Listen to me, Dallin. The Lords of Darkness do not control white magyck. You will have all your powers, although Passio may well be able to see through your cloak of invisibility. If you are injured, you will have the ability to regenerate. You will never age. Only decapitation will end your life and that of Passio. Engage the demons at your peril. They will fight as a pair. Know that they bleed as you do and feel pain. Use your wits and magyck to escape." The Lady moved closer. *"Time is running out, Dallin; do you agree to forgo true death and join the earthbound immortals?"*

Without hesitation, Dallin nodded his consent. "Yes."

"*Then I bestow upon you the armor of Arious, the strength of twenty, and the gift of immortality.*"

Black scales crept over Dallin's body from knuckles to neck. He flexed his fists and sprang to his feet. The armor moved like a second skin. "Does this come off?"

"*Aye, with a thought. However, guard your thoughts, Dallin, for now they control powerful magyck. Fight well, my champion.*" The Lady faded into a blue mist.

Dallin glanced down at Stryker. "Stand up; we have work to do." He scooped up Buzz and headed for the door. "Fancy the Loop being a dragon in disguise?"

Stryker followed in silence. Dallin had grown another six inches in height, and his body mass had increased. Immortality certainly had its rewards. Pain gripped his heart. Whatever happened today, Dallin and Lailii were lost to him forever, even if they returned from the Underworld. In a millisecond of their time, he would grow old, and they would soon lose interest in him. He shook his head, dismayed at his selfishness. His lover would fight demons today, and all he could think of was his own stupid insecurities. *Get a fucking grip. He needs me – they need me.*

Dallin dropped Buzz onto the floor and took the tunic and belt Cruz offered. He pulled the tunic over his armor, strapped on the belt, and checked the dagger and the small bottle of holy water. He slipped his dirk into the scabbard concealed in his boot, and then attached a leather helm to his belt. His brothers had said little during his explanation of the Lady's plan.

"I wish we could go with you." Kaden slapped Dallin on the back.

"Then he would fail." Stryker replied. "His talent will hide him from the guards. We must have faith in the Lady's plan."

"Her plan doesn't cover a demon or two following us through the gate." Dallin frowned. "While I'm away, use Buzz to ferry as much fire power as the Gate plateau can carry. Have my men fully aware of the situation and ready to fight."

A strange calm seeped into Dallin. The years of training for battle fell into place. Fear would come, he knew, but the rush of adrenalin would soon push doubts aside. The knowledge he may die took second place to the importance of the mission. *I am the King of the Prides, I am the Lady's Champion, I will succeed.* He called Buzz to his side and bent to look into her four green eyes. "Listen to me. On your return from the Underworld, I command you to take orders from Stryker and Cruz. Now change into a dragon, and fly us to the Gate."

The Loop ran into the clearing. With a rush of wind so fierce Dallin fought to keep on his feet, Buzz exploded into a black dragon. The beast lifted its head and roared, shaking the ground and bending the treetops. Birds took to the sky, and small animals ran for cover. Dallin lifted his head to gaze at the awesome creature. Black as night, glossy scales covered her body to the tip of a long, forked tail. Spikes ran from her shoulders down the entire length of her body. The dragon's head, with blue eyes as big as lagoons, tapered to flared nostrils, and a maw filled with brilliant white teeth. Dallin grinned. "You are magnificent."

"*You should see my wings.*" Buzz dropped her head and snorted great clouds of steam.

The dragon's voice boomed in Dallin's head. Gods, he could communicate telepathically with a dragon. "Show me."

Buzz lifted her head, the scales on her long neck glistening in the early morning sunlight. With a whoosh, her wings unfurled. The gigantic bat wings felled trees and sent the remaining animal population of Demon Island running for cover.

"Holy fuck." Stryker gripped Dallin's arm. "You sure you can control that thing? You *do* remember she hates my guts, right?"

Unafraid, Dallin walked toward the dragon. "I knew she was special the day I found her." He shot a glance at Stryker. "She will do what I say. My main worry is how we get onto her back."

The dragon dropped flat on the ground. With little effort, Dallin climbed up and slid between the spikes on her back. Stryker tossed up the supplies, and then, with an anguished look, climbed up behind Dallin.

Dallin threw him a grin. "Hang on." He patted Buzz's neck. "Okay girl, take us to the Gate."

Dallin gripped the spikes, his heart thundered. The dragon crouched, and then speared into the air. They soared high above the clouds, and Demon Island became a small dot in the endless blue ocean. The dragon hovered in the freezing air. Wind filled its wings like the sails of an ancient ship. Dallin understood the joy surging through his dragon. How long had she remained imprisoned in the Loop's body? He pushed against her mind. *Soon, we will be free to ride together across the skies, but first I need you to help me rescue Lailii and my son. I will never ask you to be a Loop again if this is your wish; you have my word.*

"*I would have the best of both worlds, my prince.*" Buzz chuckled. "*On cold nights, your bed is very warm.*"

The dragon tipped to one side and soared downward. Dallin heard Stryker swear. He held his breath until they landed precariously on the side of the mountain. Buzz attached her massive body to the sheer rock face by her sharp talons. Dallin unhooked the supplies and threw them onto the small plateau in front of the Gate. He grabbed Stryker by the arm, and using his superior strength helped him onto the ledge. A cold wind whistled past their ears. They crawled along the small walkway and into a cave. "Thank the Lady, there's a cave here. Problem is, there's no room to fight if Passio follows me through the Gate."

"Leave that to me." Stryker dragged the supplies into the cave. "You should go. Gods' speed."

Dallin pulled his lover close and inhaled his rich scent. Their lips met in a tender kiss that said more than words. With a long sigh, Dallin lifted his head and met Stryker's gaze. "When you name our son, remember he is a king."

"Then I shall leave that honor to you, my king." Stryker gave Dallin an exaggerated bow. "Go get our mate."

Without a backward glance, Dallin strode back along the walkway and leapt onto the dragon's back. The beast pushed away from the cliff and soared into the air, morphing into a Terravampire. Dallin flattened his body against the smooth-skinned beast and wrapped his arms around the creature's neck, hanging on for dear life. They circled the top of the mountain, watching the changing scenes on the Gate. Passio's castle loomed in the Gate's depths, followed by the scene of the ballroom. Other vistas flashed by in three-minute intervals. As the sequence replayed,

Buzz moved skyward, her Terravampire body hovering in an updraft of wind. With unnerving accuracy, she plunged forward, entering the gate the split second it changed. They soared into the Underworld unnoticed and circled the castle.

Black clouds raced across the sky, emphasizing the misery of the place. Lightning flashed in quick succession, sending the stink of burnt earth into the air. The land of never-ending night—a fitting place for the evil housed there. Terravampires screeched, landing en masse to feed on the bodies of Passio's torture victims piled high at the postern gate. Buzz began her descent, tucking her sleek, black wings close to her sides, and then dropping unnoticed at the back of the castle. The secret passageway began under a clump of bushes beneath the fourth tower. Dallin slipped from her back. "Good girl. Go back to Stryker."

"If you need me, I will come." Buzz pushed Dallin with her nose.

Dallin watched Buzz soar into the air. Suddenly, painfully alone, he stood to his full height and glanced around. Using his cat's night vision, he counted the towers and then moved swiftly toward the clump of bushes under the fourth one. Forming a small, illumination globe, he sent the spinning ball of light into the undergrowth to seek out the entrance. He dragged the shrubs apart and squeezed into a tunnel covered with cobwebs and housing spiders bigger than his fist. The globe showed the way upward. Dallin ignored the snakes and other reptiles and began to climb the dirt path. Soil trickled down at every step; the passage was unstable and near collapse. He rounded a bend and stopped before a pile of fallen rocks. With a flick of his hand, he used magyck to push open a small aperture and crawled through on all fours.

This part of the tunnel opened up. Large flagstones covered the floor, and the walls were made of granite. Dallin shook the dust from his hair and continued. Water streamed down the walls, and the disgusting stench of death filled the air. The passageway began to break into a series of tunnels. He glanced around, not sure which way to proceed. The stench came from the tunnels to the left – the dungeons. He would move to the right in the hope the way led to the part of the castle where Passio had imprisoned Lailii. Dragging the leather helm from his belt, he stopped for a second to listen. His blood pounded in his ears. In the distance, he could hear the sound of music. He forced the helm over his head. If he ran into Passio or his friend, Kaos, would he pass for a guard?

Dallin thought of Lailii; the image of her face soothed his nerves. He straightened his shoulders and continued toward the music. The passage ended in a wall, no door, nothing. Dallin stared at the wall. *Use your talents*, the Lady had said. Drawing on his magyck, Dallin imagined the granite bricks as a cloud of smoke. Tentatively, he thrust his hand forward. To his delight, his fist passed straight through the solid wall. Without another thought, he cloaked and stepped through into a narrow hallway. The sickly scent of demon accosted his highly sensitive nose. He looked both ways. A flight of stairs led to an upper floor on the left. He turned right. Moving swiftly, he made his way along the corridor. He turned the corner and barely avoided colliding into two guards hovering at the entrance to the ballroom. To his relief, they stared straight through him.

The binding spell formed in his mind. He would have to use this incantation with care. The guards must remain standing upright. Another idea came to him. Not the binding spell — the fast-freeze charm. Dallin rubbed his chin, and then smiled at his own creativity. He moved between the guards and stood in the middle of the ballroom. Another four guards surrounded the Gate. With a flick of his hand, Dallin cast the spell. De-cloaking, he stood for a few seconds to get his bearings. Now he had secured the guards, cloaking would only alert Passio to his presence.

Fourth door from the vestibule. Dallin walked slowly along the passageway toward the foyer. Passio appeared from a doorway and glared at him, his red eyes blazing. Dallin froze mid step. He cast his eyes downward; his fingers tingled with magyck. He braced for action.

"Not here, you fool." Passio brushed past him, and then braced his hand against the wall. "I said to guard the fourth door from the vestibule."

Dallin could not believe his luck. Passio moved slowly, weaving from side to side. Dallin smiled. The pig must have consumed Lailii's tainted blood. He followed the demon at a distance. He may well pass as a guard, but Passio would certainly recognize his scent if he got too close. As directed, he moved into position in front of a door on the other side of the vestibule. Dallin glanced around. No other men guarded this area.

"Remain here. Don't allow the female to leave this room." Passio turned and walked unsteadily toward the music.

The demon headed toward the ballroom — with the Gate. Damn. If he could take Lailii from this room, they had no chance of escape. He turned the copper doorknob and slowly pushed open the door. Lailii scrambled off the bed, her beautiful face streaked with tears. She looked lost and defeated. A lump formed in Dallin's throat. He held out a hand. "It's me, little one, Dallin."

"I'm not fooled by you, Kaos. Go away." Lailii backed against the wall.

Dallin ripped off his helm and opened his arms. "I came to you in your dreams. Come here and smell me. I promise I don't stink like a fucking demon."

"I don't trust you." Lailii wrapped her arms around her stomach. "My Dallin isn't as big as you. Go away."

"Do you remember when we first met?" Dallin pushed down the urge to run to her, and smiled. "I thought you were a child and stripped you naked. You sure told me where to go. Then you gave me the spiel about cursing me if I raped you." He moved closer. "I was your first, and I love you with all my heart." With a sigh, he caught a tear running down her cheek on his fingertip. "We should never have left you. Father said you were well, but I gather he never gave you our messages. I sent mother away. No one will interfere with our lives now. Come home with me, little one."

"Dallin, is that really you?" Lailii took a step toward him.

Dallin pulled her into his arms and buried his face in her hair. "Gods, Lailii, I thought you were dead. The Lady said you were immortal; I didn't believe her."

"Immortal? Me?" Lailii stared up at him blankly.

With a frown, Dallin met her gaze. "You are the earthbound daughter of the Lady. That's why Passio craves your blood. It contains white magyck and allows him to walk above ground for longer periods of time."

"Why did the Lady subject me to such hardship?" Lailii's fingers clutched Dallin's tunic.

"Who knows? I'm sure She had her reasons." He bent his head to seek her lips. So soft, Lailii pressed against him. Dallin held her close and feasted on her delicious mouth. With difficulty, he drew away and stared into her eyes. "Our cub, is he safe?"

"Yes, and not detected." Lailii placed a hand on her belly. "He grows stronger by the day."

Placing his hand over Lailii's, he smiled. "He is a great king in the making." He frowned. "We need to go. I've disabled the guards, but we don't have too much time before Passio discovers they're frozen. He was heading toward the ballroom last time I saw him."

"You saw Passio, and he didn't do anything?" Lailii's eyes flashed. "Good—then the spell I put on my blood is working, although I'm not sure how long it will disable the demons. They should have fallen asleep, they are more powerful than I imagined." She looked up at Dallin. "Kiss me again; my powers are low. Passio broke his word and drank twice as much this morning. My blood makes him irrational."

Dallin pushed her gently against the wall and found her mouth. His hands slid under her top and teased her swollen breasts. She moaned in his mouth and kissed him back, twisting her body against him. From beneath his lashes, Dallin watched the glow emanate from her body. He squeezed her hard nipples, inhaled her feminine arousal, and his cock grew hard. With a groan, he pulled away and looked down at her damp lips. Gods, he loved her mouth. "I want you so bad, but we must go."

Reaching down, he pulled the dirk from his boot and handed it to her. "Magyck may be useless against the demons. We can injure them—the Lady told me they bleed and feel pain—but decapitation is the only way to kill them. If necessary, strike the blade in the neck, thigh, or groin to slow them."

"You don't have a weapon." Lailii took the dirk and concealed it in the pocket of her skirt. "There are swords on the wall in the ballroom."

He touched her face, running his thumb across her bottom lip. "I have a fine dagger and my magyck. I don't think we will just walk out of here, little one. Promise me something. When I engage the demons, run for the Gate, look for Stryker on the other side, and go to him. Don't look back."

Lailii looked at her mate in disbelief. She shook her head. "I promised to be by your side for eternity. I am a Spellweaver. I will fight beside my prince."

"Not this time." Dallin shook his head. "Save our son. Do this for me."

With a sigh, Lailii met Dallin's gaze. "I will save our son." She glanced toward the open door. "I hear footsteps. Replace your helm, and go stand by the door."

After taking a deep breath, Lailii moved to the foot of the bed and faced Dallin. *Please let this work.* She raised her voice and articulated each word. "Take me to Passio. Why don't you understand?"

Passio hung in the doorway like a bat, his fangs stained with blood. Lailii shivered. She stamped her foot in an effort to appear annoyed and pouted. "I asked this lout to take me to you, and he just stands there like an idiot."

"You draw me like a moth destined to die in the flame of a candle." Passio lurched forward. "Your blood is the finest aphrodisiac I've ever experienced, although, it intoxicates me to the point of apoplexy."

Moving slowly toward him, Lailii forced a smile. "Your bite makes me needy. I am wet from your last visit."

The expression on Passio's face would have been comical if the circumstances had not been so grave. Not waiting for his reply, Lailii continued. "I would have you and Kaos in my bed. I find I crave you both. However, you have depleted my magyck, and I yearn to listen to the sweet music coming through the walls and watch the passage of the scenes on your Gate."

"If you lie, I will beat you." Passio turned her and bent her over the bed. "Wet, you say?"

Lailii's hand went to the dirk in her pocket. Forced face down over the end of the bed, she prayed silently Dallin would remain motionless. Passio pulled her skirts up and kicked open her legs. She turned to face him. "You gave your word you would never rape me."

Passio's icy cold fingers caressed her pussy, and then dipped inside. He gave a maniacal laugh and dragged her to her feet.

She turned to glare at him. "Was that really necessary?"

"Oh, yes." Passio slowly licked his fingers. "You are so wet—have you pined for me?"

"Since you left, I have thought of little else but you and Kaos."

"I knew you would come to your senses." He swayed drunkenly and offered his arm. "Come and feast on beauty, and later, I will bring Kaos to your room, and we will gorge ourselves on you." He escorted Lailii from the room. He paused in the hall and turned his red gaze to Dallin. "Follow me. You will escort Lailii back to her room in a little while."

Dallin bit down hard on his cheek. To stand and watch Passio touch his mate had made his blood boil. They must get to the ballroom. If he attacked the demon now, Lailii did not have a chance. Passio would break her in half without a second thought. His stomach knotted. Had the demons fucked her? What else had she endured in Passio's company? He would kill the filthy pigs. Grinding his teeth, he followed them into the ballroom. Passio guided Lailii to the Gate and stood behind her, grinning like a monkey. Then he lifted her hand and sank his sharp fangs into her wrist. The demon's eyes glazed over with pleasure. Dallin saw the glint of the dirk in Lailii's hand. A second later, Kaos entered the ballroom, his collar spotted with blood.

The knife flashed. Lailii struck like a snake, repeatedly driving the blade into Passio's groin. The demon howled with pain, clutching his balls. Dallin spun around and dragged a sword from the display. He turned to see Kaos running forward, screaming at the guards.

"He can shield himself with white magyck." Passio gurgled. "Use your sword."

Kaos screamed a battle cry and produced a sword out of thin air. He danced toward Dallin, uttering a string of expletives. In the middle of the ballroom, Passio slipped to the floor, a look of shocked astonishment on his face. The demon's thin arm clung tightly around Lailii's neck, dragging her to the blood-soaked floor. Lailii, platinum hair stained red, continued to stab with the dirk, attacking Passio's neck with gusto. Blood covered her bare legs, and her small feet slipped constantly in the crimson flow. Dallin felt a rush of pride. No female had fought so valiantly beside him. He had no doubt Lailii could keep Passio occupied; the demon had gorged on her poisoned blood.

Dallin lifted his sword and parried Kaos' first bone-shattering hit. Swords slid, the razor-sharp blades screaming. Even drugged, the demon had incredible strength. Dallin broke free and brought his weapon down hard. Kaos met his blow with the aplomb of an expert. They began the deadly game of attack and retreat. The practiced dance of life and death every swordsman knew by heart. They circled, then struck, testing each other's strengths and weaknesses. Swords crossed with another shriek of metal on metal. They pushed hard against each other and stared, like two mad stags, their faces a breath apart. Magyck tingled in Dallin's fist. He hit Kaos in the side of his head with every ounce of strength and white magic he could muster. The blow hit with a crack of bone. The demon rolled back on his heels and crashed to the floor, his sword spinning across the polished wooden surface.

Lailii's fingers slipped on the bloody handle of the dirk. To her horror, Passio began to regenerate.

The next moment, she slid across the floor, landing in front of the Gate. Dallin stood over Kaos, breathing heavily.

Pressing a hand over her mouth in horror, Lailii watched Passio drag his bloodstained body to his knees. The demon swayed, got to his feet, and stalked toward Dallin.

She screamed. "Dallin, behind you."

Lailii studied the scenes flashing past in the Gate. She held up her hand and formed a spell in her mind. The instant she saw Stryker through the portal, she sent her magyck to pause the Gate's cycle. She turned and met Dallin's gaze. How could she leave him?

"I will take your pretty head with the same blade as I used on your sire." Passio laughed and sent a bolt of lightning at Dallin.

To Lailii's relief, Dallin lifted his barrier in time to prevent injury, but the force knocked him off his feet. Gods, Passio was growing stronger by the second.

"At least I'm willing to die like a man." Dallin sprung to his feet. "You fight with magyck. Are you afraid you will lose if we meet on an even field?"

Heart pounding, Lailii glanced from one to the other. The men began to circle each other, readying for combat. From the other side of the Gate, Stryker pleaded, urging her to leave. On the floor, Kaos began to move, slowly gaining consciousness. Biting her bottom lip, Lailii wiped the dripping handle of the dirk on her dress. Keeping her back to the wall, she inched slowly past the fight, and then ran toward Kaos. The semi-conscious demon tried to roll away from her attack, his arms flailing. She rolled with him, driving the dirk into his neck. Hot, crimson blood poured down her chest and splattered over her face. Kaos' red eyes faded to green and rolled back in his head. She crawled away. Across the ballroom, Passio, laughing like a maniac, had Dallin pressed against the wall, their swords locked. The muscles in Dallin's arms bunched with the strain of holding the demon's blade from his throat.

"Go." Dallin yelled at Lailii. "For our son."

Fighting the lump in her throat, Lailii ran for the Gate.

Stryker caught Lailii and carried her into the cave. He set her down and pressed a bottle of water into her hand. "Stay here."

"Passio will kill him." Lailii sobbed. "We have to do something." She lifted her face to the heavens. "Dear Lady, I beg you, save my mate, your champion, from the demon. He is brave and loyal; don't let him die like this."

Stryker ran back to the Gate. Dallin, his face a mask of determination, forced Passio back, using brute force. The demon struck again, his blade slicing across Dallin's armor and ripping the tunic from his body. Dark spirals of smoke began to dance around the room. Dallin began to choke as the dark magyck poured into his lungs. Passio stood back, grinning, as if waiting for Dallin to fall. Stryker's hands formed into fists, and he took a step forward.

"You will die if you proceed."

"Then he won't die alone." Stryker said without hesitation. But then . . . . *Who had spoken?*

He spun around. Time stood still. *Arious!*

Stryker fell to his knees before the god of war, the father of all the Prides. The man stood seven feet tall and bore a striking resemblance to Dallin. Stryker bowed his head. "I am humbled, great one."

"Being humble won't help my mate's champion. Although, I'm sure the Great One will scold me for my interference. The Prides have come a long way since I created the first shifter. Tell my Prides how proud I am of your progress." He turned to Lailii. "Child, know that we never deserted you. Boda placed you here to enhance the Prides. Long ago, your mother paired another Spellweaver with her first champion for the same reason. They are the immortals that rule the Lands of the Five Gates in the Second Dimension." He turned to Stryker, drew his sword, and dropped it blade first into a small patch of grass before the cave. "Take the Sword of Vengeance.

Throw it through the Gate to Dallin so he may rid the world of Lord Passio." The god faded into the breeze.

Stryker jumped to his feet. He grabbed Vengeance and ran toward the Gate.

"Don't go through." Lailii rushed to his side. "Do as he says, and throw Dallin the sword."

Dallin gasped for breath. His sword slipped from his grasp, and he waited for the deathblow. The cold wall pressed against his sweat-soaked back. Passio's blade pushed against his throat, and the warm wetness of his own blood trickled down his chest. It would be over soon. His gaze flicked toward the Gate for one last look at his mates. Stryker, his face ashen, stood at the Gate and held up a golden sword encrusted with jewels—he recognized it immediately from castle paintings. The mythical Vengeance? Sword of Arious. Could it be true?

With his last ounce of strength, he forced Passio's blade from his neck and reached for the dagger at his waist. He plunged the blade into

Passio's thigh repeatedly. The demon screeched and stumbled back. Stryker yelled something undistinguishable, his voice an eerie echo, and then threw the sword through the Gate.

Dallin lifted his arm. Vengeance flew hilt over tip, landing heavily in his hand. A rush of power surged through him until his ears hummed with magyck. He dragged off his helm and threw it to the floor. Passio regenerated in seconds and stalked forward. Dallin gripped the perfectly balanced blade and turned to one side to face his opponent. The demon danced forward, slashing his sword. With one sweep, Dallin sliced off the demigod's right arm. Passio gazed at him with disbelief, and then looked down at his dismembered limb still clutching the weapon.

"That was for killing my father."

Dallin sliced off Passio's other arm. "That was for touching my mate."

Behind him, Kaos got to his feet. Dallin spun around and sliced him in half. He turned back to

Passio. "This is for mankind." With one blow, he decapitated the demon.

Lifting his chin, Dallin skirted the pools of blood on the floor and headed for the Gate. He stepped out of the Underworld, glad to feel the sunshine on his face. He hugged Stryker and dragged Lailii into his arms. "Passio is dead. You were so brave, little one." He kissed her hair. "You weaved a spell to freeze the Gate. Do you have another to seal it?"

"Yes, the magyck of the Prides surges through me." She turned and threw a spell at the Gate. Then she rested her hand on Dallin's arm and looked up at him. "You do know Kaos will regenerate, don't you?"

Dallin looked down at her blood-splattered face and frowned. "Gods, I should have taken his head."

"It will take him a while to open more Gates." Stryker glanced behind him into the blackened Gate. "Won't it?"

With a shrug, Dallin pulled them close. "We'll deal with that if and when the time comes." He met Stryker's gaze. "Call the dragon; we're going home."

Epilogue

Dallin stood at the open window. The scent of roses drifted up from the garden below. Moonlight flowed into the room, casting velvet shadows across the rug. He gazed down at his son. They had decided to call him Alaric. With the black hair of the Vane and the curls of the Talynx, the Lady had blessed him with the combined looks of both fathers. Dallin kissed the infant's pink cheek and touched the black hair that stuck up in every direction. Alaric gazed up at him with the opalescent eyes of the Vane flecked with green and silver. Pure, white magyck glowed from this grandchild of the Lady. He would become the most powerful of all the Vane. Dallin smiled and pressed a kiss to his cheek. He gazed at Lailii, sleeping peacefully in Stryker's arms, and his heart filled with joy.

So much had happened these past weeks. As king of the Vane, he had passed new laws and made plans to visit all the Prides of the Nine Gates. The demon threat would never be over, and he needed to discuss plans for the future safety of the realms.

Revelation of Lailii's identity and her immortality, not to mention his own, had brought mixed reactions. He knew Stryker feared growing old and passing through the veil alone. The thought of watching his mate and brothers die filled him with trepidation. He lifted Alaric onto his shoulder and began to pat the cub's back. What could he do? His son would never become king, as he would never die. Perhaps, he would tire of being king and abdicate?

That sounded a fair proposition, but losing Stryker would tear him apart.

The air shimmered, and the Lady materialized in a blue haze. The Lady made frequent visits to see Alaric. *Heaven's above, I'll never get used to having the goddess for a mother-in-law.* Dallin drew Alaric close to his chest. "Forgive me for not kneeling, dear Lady."

"*You are troubled?*" The Lady's face creased into a frown. "*I bound you and Stryker for all eternity. Think you I would take him from you?*"

Dallin met the Lady's gaze. "You made me immortal. He will die."

"*I would not be so cruel.*" She smiled benevolently. "*Stryker and all your cubs are immortals. The Great One is most pleased with you. He has granted you the ability to bestow immortality on those you think worthy.*"

"That is a great responsibility." Dallin shook his head. "Kings will rule for thousands of years, and no progress will be made. How can it work? We'll be falling over each other."

"Not so, I gave this gift to another a long time ago and their Pride thrives in harmony. There are millions of realms for immortals to rule, Dallin. There are dimensions similar to this one that need your help. My people need the knowledge of the Vane. Send your brothers and your sons to explore new realms and bring all under the love and guidance of the Great One. Set into place rules of succession. The Fae do much the same, and they are most willing to guide you."

Dallin lifted his son from his shoulder and cradled him in his arms. "How do I find these realms?"

"Lailii is a Spellweaver; she will show you the way." The Lady laughed. *"You will be a great king, Dallin. Learn to trust in your own judgment. Your new life has just begun, and it will be a fantastic journey."* She faded into a blue mist and then vanished.

Dallin glanced down at his son. His precious cub was finally asleep. He walked across the room to lay him down in a crib beside the bed. Tenderly, he wrapped him in a blanket. He kissed Alaric's head, and then gazed at his mates sleeping so peacefully. He sighed. The Lady had granted his wish; his mates would be beside him for eternity. Gods, for the first time in his life, he understood contentment. He smiled into the darkness. Life had just become a completely new ballgame.

~The End~

About the Author

H.C. Brown a multi-published author of many genres and lives in Australia.

She welcomes feedback from her readers and answers all emails. She believes every story should have a happy ending.

Learn more about H.C. Brow online, at her blog. http://www.hcbrownauthoroferoticromance.blogspot.com

~***~

If you enjoyed Shifters and Demons, you might also like the following books from H.C. Brown and Noble Romance Publishing.

Purr-fect Seduction

Jill Morfranna, a sassy redhead from New York, is enjoying a photo shoot in the Scottish Highlands when she stumbles into an alternate realm. Trapped in a frightening world of strange creatures, her life turns upside down when a sinfully handsome shape-shifter kidnaps her. Will she win Dare of Knight Watch's heart or will he trade her for his sister at the next slave auction?

A Savage Lust

Prince Rio of Knight Watch's mission is to visit London, to retrieve the Lady's Book of Knowledge. He encounters Humans for the first time and his life freefalls into chaos. Torn between his love for a magnificent Fae male and an unusual Human female, he must complete his task or fall foul of Nox, King of the Faerie.

LaVergne, TN USA
23 March 2011
221399LV00001B/29/P

9 781605 922621